The Diamond Girls

I feel very fond of all my Diamond girls and think they're a fantastic family, though maybe I'm glad they don't live next door to me! I was prodded into action to write their story by a Christmas newspaper feature. Various celebrities were asked to name the worst book they'd ever read. I was idly leafing through this over my breakfast when I suddenly spotted the title of one of *my* books, *The Illustrated Mum*. A well-known politician chose this as her worst book ever, partly because she said the two sisters in the book had different fathers. I thought this was so bizarre I laughed out loud. Why on earth would anyone think this a reason for disliking a children's book? How can children help it, anyway, if they've got different fathers? I wanted to show by the end of the story that their family is warm and caring and loving in spite of their chaotic lifestyle, while Dixie's little friend Mary in her neat mock-Tudor villa comes from a very cold and troubled background.

Dixie's the youngest sister, the gentle dreamy girl who tells the story. She's my favourite Diamond girl, though I also have a very soft spot for Jude. My best friend gave me the idea for Dixie's toy budgie Bluebell. We were talking about the pets we'd longed for when we were children, and she said she'd longed for a budgerigar but her mum wouldn't let her have one. She'd therefore bought a plastic budgie from a pet shop and walked round with it perched on her finger, pretending it was real. I liked this story so much I had to let my Dixie do exactly that.

I made much of the horrors of moving house in *The Diamond Girls* – and almost as soon as it was published *I* moved house too. I had more friends to help me than poor Sue Diamond, but it was still pretty traumatic – especially as I have around 15,000 books! But now I'm happily settled in my lovely new house, with all my books in specially built beautiful bookcases. My Diamond girls might decide to move away from the Planet Estate but I intend to stay exactly where I am for ever!

Jacqueline Wilson

The Diamond Girls

Jacqueline Wilson

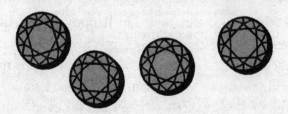

Illustrated by Nick Sharratt

CORGI BOOKS

THE DIAMOND GIRLS
A CORGI BOOK 978 0552 55612 5

First published in Great Britain by Doubleday
an imprint of Random House Children's Books

Doubleday edition published 2004
First Corgi edition published 2005
This Corgi edition published 2007

5 7 9 10 8 6 4

Set in Century School Book

Addresses for companies within The Random House Group Limited can be
found at: www.randomhouse.co.uk/offices.htm

THE RANDOM HOUSE GROUP Limited Reg. No. 954009
www.kidsatrandomhouse.co.uk

A CIP catalogue record for this book is available from the British Library.

Printed in the UK by CPI Bookmarque, Croydon, CR0 4TD

For Nick and Jon

1

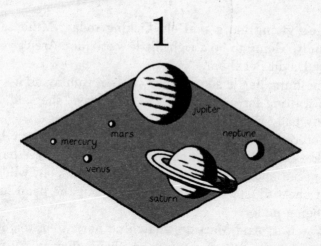

'I've got a surprise for you girls,' said Mum. 'We're moving.'

We all stared at her. She was flopping back in her chair, slippered feet propped right up on the kitchen table amongst the cornflake bowls, tummy jutting over her skirt like a giant balloon. She didn't look capable of moving herself as far as the front door. Her scuffed fluffy mules could barely support her weight. Maybe she needed hot air underneath her and then she'd rise gently upwards and float out of the open window.

'Quit staring at my stomach, Dixie,' Mum snapped.

'How can she *help* staring?' said Jude. 'It's so gross.'

'Oh yuck, it's *moving*!' Rochelle squealed.

Mum cradled her tummy, patting the little bulgy bit wiggling about beneath her navel. I hoped it wouldn't wiggle too much. Mum's navel looked ready to pop out like a cork.

I used to think that's how babies were born. That was weird enough. The real explanation seems worse. I'm sure I don't want any babies myself, ever.

'He's giving me a real old kicking today,' Mum said proudly. 'Going to be a right little footballer. Aren't you, baby David Beckham?'

She hung her head over her swollen tummy as if she was waiting for an answer. '*Yes, Mummy!*' she said, in a tiny baby voice.

'You're nuts, Mum,' said Jude. 'You've been a bit bonkers ever since you knew the baby was a boy. What's so special about *boys*?' Jude threw her arms out wildly, as if she'd like to whack every boy about the head just for being male.

'Watch it,' said Martine, snatching her cup of tea out of Jude's way. 'What are you on about anyway, Mum? We don't want to move again. We've played musical chairs all round the blooming Bletchworth Estate.'

We started off in South Block. We moved there when a three-bedroom flat became vacant, but then Mum had a row with the people on our landing. We swapped to the ground floor of North Block, but it was so damp we had rotten colds and coughs all winter, so then we moved up to the top floor. It wasn't a good idea to be right under the roof. Whenever it rained Jude and I had to squeeze into Mum's room because we had too many leaks coming through our ceiling. The council never came to get it fixed no matter how many times we phoned.

We liked living there even so.

Martine liked living on the top floor because her boyfriend Tony lived right next door in number 113. Martine's the oldest of us Diamond girls. She's just sixteen. She says that makes her an adult and she can do whatever she likes. She looks exactly like Mum but she tries very hard not to. She's got Mum's lovely thick black hair but Martine dyes hers blonde. Mum likes to wear short skirts so Martine wears jeans, low slung so you can see the top of her thong when she bends forwards.

Jude liked living on the top floor because she knew how to get through a secret trapdoor onto the roof. She claimed it as her own private territory. Lots of the boys in our block wanted to climb up there too but Jude wouldn't let them. She can get the better of all the boys, even though she's smallish and only fourteen. She might be small but she's squat and very very tough. Jude looks out for me and squashes people flat if they start teasing me. We're not supposed to have favourites in our family but if I did have a favourite sister then it's definitely Jude.

Rochelle liked living on the top floor because Martine was round at Tony's so often she generally had the bedroom to herself. She could prance around pretending to be a pop singer, hairbrush for a mike, watching herself in the wardrobe mirror. She's always watching herself. I suppose I'd want to watch myself if I looked like Rochelle. She's only twelve but she tries to look much older. She's very pretty with long curly blonde hair and a heart-shaped face and pink pouty lips like one of those loveheart sweets. There is absolutely nothing else sweet about her. A lot of the time I simply can't stick my sister Rochelle.

I liked living on the top floor because I could stare out the window and pretend Bluebell and I were flying over the rooftops, high above the tower blocks, over the ocean, all the way across the world to Bluebell's birthplace in Australia. I knew that was where real budgerigars came

3

from. When I made Bluebell talk she always started off saying, 'G'day, Dixie.' However, if you were rude enough to look up Bluebell's bottom she had this little white label saying 'MADE IN CHINA'. She didn't talk Chinese but I sometimes fished out left-over cartons of chow mein and chop suey from the dustbins and Bluebell dug her beak in very happily.

I felt for Bluebell up my cardie sleeve. I didn't often walk round with her perched on my finger now, even at home, because everyone acted as if I was a total nutcase. I stuffed her up my sleeve instead like a little paper hankie. I gave her feathers a secret stroke every now and then. I needed to stroke her now because Martine and Jude and Rochelle were all shouting and I knew it bothered her.

'We want to stay here, Mum, OK?' said Jude, sticking out her chin. 'North Block's much the best. South Block sucks. *And* Middle Block. North Block's my *territory*.'

'I've got my bedroom just the way I like it,' said Rochelle. 'It's not fair, Mum – you never think about us.'

'We can't leave this flat, not now Tony helped do it up so swish,' said Martine. He just helped her paint her and Rochelle's bedroom but she acted like he did a complete *Changing Rooms*. 'We'll never get as good a flat, not on this estate.'

'You're right,' said Mum. She eased her legs down onto the floor, rubbing at her big blue veins. Then she sat up as straight as she could and folded her arms across her big bosom. She gave us such a look that we all shut up, even Jude.

'We're not getting a better flat on this estate, OK? We're moving, like I said. It's all planned, in all my star

4

charts. Every time I read the tarot cards the wheel of fortune comes up, symbolizing a new beginning. We have to act on it. It's like our destiny.'

'You and your stupid fortune-telling, Mum. You're like a blooming gypsy. *My* fortune's right here,' said Martine.

'There are too many bad vibes here,' said Mum, shifting on her chair and patting her tummy protectively.

'Yeah, and whose fault is that?' said Jude. 'Why did you ever have to get pregnant again?'

'I can't help fate, darling. It's all in the stars.' Mum looked up, as if the Milky Way was shining across our kitchen ceiling.

'We did a project on the stars at school. And the planets and all their little moons. We had to draw them but my compass didn't work so mine went all wobbly,' I said.

'I did that project when I was back in primary school. I got an A,' said Rochelle.

'Why do you always have to show off, Rochelle?' I said. 'Who cares about your stupid A grades?'

I cared. It was horribly unfair that Rochelle got to be very pretty *and* very clever. Jude wasn't pretty but she was very clever, even though she didn't try much at school. Martine was pretty but she wasn't any good at lessons and couldn't wait to leave.

I was plain and most people thought I was stupid.

'Pipe down, girls. Now listen. We're going to have a fresh start. We're leaving this old dump altogether.'

'No we're not,' said Jude, folding her arms too. 'You can't make us.'

'Oh yes, we are moving,' said Mum, and she nodded at the letter in front of her.

We'd all thought it was just another bill or some silly

letter from the social. We hadn't taken any notice when Mum was reading it, though I had wondered why she hadn't scrumpled it up and thrown it in the rubbish bin.

Martine snatched the letter. 'The Planet Estate?' she read.

'Isn't it just perfect?' said Mum. 'See, Jude, it's fate.'

'Oh my God, it's not even in London! We can't go there. How can I see Tony?'

'I think you've been seeing way too much of that Tony, if you must know,' said Mum. 'You're too young to get serious.'

'Oh, that's great, coming from you! You had me when you were – what, sixteen?'

'That's my point, I know what I'm talking about.'

'You're moving us all to some weird estate in the middle of nowhere just to split Tony and me up?' Martine wailed, starting to cry.

'Oh for God's sake, stop being such a drama queen! The whole world doesn't revolve around you and your boyfriend. I'm doing this for all of us. We need a bigger place, now you're all having a little brother.' Mum patted her stomach.

She said it as if we'd all begged for a brother. We'd all been appalled and embarrassed when she told us she was going to have another baby.

'You can't *get* bigger than three-bedroom flats, not council,' said Jude.

'I've got my whole bedroom wall like this big pop collage. It'll ruin it if I have to tear it all down,' said Rochelle.

'You can make another one. You'll have more space. We're moving to a *house*,' said Mum. 'A proper family house with our own garden.'

6

We all missed a beat, taking it in. I clutched Bluebell.
'Will we be allowed pets?' I asked.

'Yes, Dixie.'

'Real ones? Birds?' I saw a green garden of trees with
red and purple parrots and yellow canaries and blue
budgerigars flying freely, cheeping and calling. Bluebell
quivered, trying to stretch her faded feathers.

'OK, if you're having a bird I'll have a big fluffy cat,'
said Rochelle. 'I'll have *lots* of those Persian cats with
white fur. I'll call them Snowy and Sugar Lump and Ice
Cream and Ivory.'

Phantom cats, as big and white as polar bears, were
stalking through my garden, climbing the trees,
pouncing on all my helpless rainbow birds.

Jude saw me clutching my sleeve. 'And *I'll* get a big
Rottweiler and he'll swat those pesky cats with one blow
of his big paws. Then I'll put him on a lead and he'll be
our guard dog and he'll always look out for you, Dixie,'
said Jude.

'What are you on about?' said Martine, still crying.
'This is just crazy talk – dogs and cats and bogging
budgies. It isn't a *game*. We can't move. I *won't*!'

'Yes you will,' said Mum. 'Stop shouting at me! I don't
want my blood pressure going up, it's bad for the baby.'

'That *badword* baby,' said Martine. She said so many
badwords we all blinked.

'Stop that!' said Mum. 'I won't have it, do you hear? I
know you're just upset because of Tony. You can't really
think that about your poor little baby brother.'

'Yes I do!' Martine shrieked. 'You're so selfish, Mum.
You act like none of us girls matter. You're just so
obsessed with wanting a stupid boy you're mucking up

all our lives. You should hear what they say about us on the estate – what they say about *you*.'

'Well, I won't have to hear, because we're moving. You can swear at me all you like but it's settled and signed for, totally official,' said Mum, rolling up the letter and smacking it on the table. She hit her wrist by mistake and rubbed it furiously. 'Ouch! Now look what you made me do.'

'Good!' Martine shouted and she marched out, slamming the front door.

'As if I care what those boring old bags have been saying about me,' said Mum, having a sip of her tea. 'Anyway, what *have* they been saying?'

I looked at Jude and Rochelle. Rochelle opened her big mouth but Jude gave her a quick nudge.

'So, this Planet Estate . . .' Jude said to distract Mum. 'How did you hear about it?'

People are always saying things about her, but we don't tell Mum, even when we're mad at her.

'I went down the council telling them all about the baby, wanting a swap, and this girl diddled away at her computer and the moment she mentioned the Planet Estate I had this weird tight feeling in my chest—'

'Indigestion,' said Jude.

'*Intuition!* I just knew it was the place for us, especially when she said that all six blocks also had streets of houses with gardens, for big families.'

Rochelle was counting on her fingers. 'Six blocks? There are *nine* planets – I remember from when we did them at school.'

'Yeah, you'd better get off to school, you're all late,' said Mum.

'No point going though, is there? Not if we're moving,' said Jude.

'You bunk off half the time anyway, you bad girl,' said Mum. 'Well, you can make yourself useful going down to Tesco and bringing back as many cardboard boxes as you can manage. We'll need them for packing.'

'*I'm* going to school,' said Rochelle. 'I'm telling all my friends we're moving. We're really going to be living in a proper house with a garden, Mum? Can I have my very own bedroom? It's not fair I always have to share.'

We *all* share. We started off Martine and Jude, and Rochelle and me, but it didn't work. It's better with Martine and Rochelle, and Jude and me. But it would be best if we all had our own bedrooms.

'Can I have my own bedroom too, Mum? Can all of us?' I asked.

'We'll have to see, darling. Maybe. I don't know exactly how many rooms there are, or how big they are.'

'I bags the biggest bedroom,' said Rochelle.

'No, no, I've got to have that for me and the baby. I've been thinking about taking out another loan. I hate all that cheap second-hand crap. Who wants gungy old stuff for their little baby son, eh? I saw this cot with a cute little blue bear motif—'

Mum was off on one of her baby-boy rants. She'd be talking Mothercare catalogue for the next ten minutes. Jude yawned, poured herself another bowl of cornflakes and went to watch one of her *Buffy* videos on the telly. She pulled her school tie off, rolled up her shirt sleeves and kicked off her shoes.

Rochelle packed her school bag ostentatiously, playing at being the good little girl.

9

I was still trying to think of nine planets. I hadn't really been concentrating when we'd studied them at school. I'd been too busy dreaming up my own planet. Bluebell and I lived there all alone in perfect peace. There'd be hardly any gravity on Planet Dixie so I could fly just like Bluebell. We shared a special mossy nest at the top of the tallest tree. It bore multi-fruit all the year round, apples on one branch, pears on another. Raspberries and blackberries and strawberries grew in leafy clumps around the trunk and grape vines dangled downwards, so that we didn't have to leave our nest to peck at breakfast.

'Dixie! Close your mouth! Stop that daydreaming, you look gormless,' Mum snapped.

'I was just trying to think of all the planets, Mum.'

'We're going to live in Mercury. Then there's Venus, Mars, Jupiter, Neptune and Saturn.'

'They've left out Pluto and Uranus,' said Rochelle.

'Yeah, well, who'd want to live in Mickey Mouse's dog or something that sounds very rude,' I said. I was still counting. 'So what's the last planet?'

'Earth, stupid. Where we live. Though you're generally on a different planet altogether, Dixie. Planet Loony.' Rochelle stuck out her tongue and made for the door.

'Hang on, Rochelle, take Dixie with you.'

'Oh *Mum*. I haven't got time to do a blooming school run. I'm *late*,' Rochelle said, on her way to the bathroom.

'I don't want to go to school today, Mum. Like Jude said, there's no point, not if we really *are* moving to this Planet place.'

'You'll get me into trouble,' said Mum, but she reached out for me and cuddled me into her. I leaned against her, though I was careful not to touch her tummy.

10

'OK, OK, little Dix, you can stay off school today.'

'Hurray!'

'Why don't you like school, eh?'

I shrugged. There was no point getting started.

'Who's your teacher? Is she giving you a hard time? You tell her it's not *your* fault you're a bit of a dilly-dream, it's just the way you were born.'

'Mmm,' I said, playing with Mum's hair.

It wasn't the teacher, it was the other kids. This girl had spotted me whispering into my cardie cuff and she'd pounced on Bluebell. She told all the others and they all did budgie squawks and screwed their fingers into their foreheads and called me Birdbrain.

'Well, you'll be at a new school soon when we're living in Mercury. It's the smallest planet, always associated with children – and here I'll be, having my baby boy in Mercury. Come to that, I've always liked Freddie Mercury too,' said Mum, chuckling. She sighed when I looked blank. 'You know, the singer with all the teeth in Queen. Freddie . . . How about that for the baby's name? Or what about Mercury?'

'If you call the poor kid Mercury he'll be teased rotten,' Jude called.

'Call him Justin,' said Rochelle, coming out the bathroom. 'Or Craig. Or Robbie.'

'I want something really special. Unusual,' said Mum.

'What other singers do I like?' said Rochelle. 'I know, Baby Busted!' She cackled with laughter and rushed off to school.

I relaxed and started plaiting Mum's long black hair.

'Help me think up a good name, Dixie. I tried hard with you girls. You're all so lucky – dead individual.

11

There aren't any other Martines or Judes or Rochelles or Dixies round here. I'm stuck with stupid old Sue. There are *heaps* of Sues.'

'There's only one of you, though, Mum,' I said. I finished one plait and tied it with a piece of string from the kitchen drawer, adding a few paperclips too as silver decoration.

'What are you doing? Turning me into whatshername – Pocahontas?' Mum said.

'Hey, you could spell your name differently. S-i-o-u-x, like the native American tribe. *That's* individual,' I said.

'Oh well, I'll give it a thought. Hey, leave off now, it's making me go all itchy. What about cowboy names for the baby?' Mum thought. 'Butch Cassidy?'

'Yeah, but what if he's a bit little and wimpy, Mum? You can't call him Butch.'

'The Sundance Kid? Hey, Sundance, that's a glorious name! And the sun is a perfect symbol of male energy, right? Little baby, are you Sundance?'

Mum put her hands on her tummy, peering at it intently, as if she could see the baby inside dancing in the sun.

I got packed in a jiffy. I crammed my clothes into one big carrier bag. They got a bit squashed but I didn't care. I don't like my clothes much. They've mostly been Rochelle's before me and she likes pink and glitter, tight skimpy stuff that shows off her figure. I haven't *got* a figure. I'm so small that even miniskirts come way past my knees, I'm so skinny that everything looks baggy on me, and I'm so pale that pink makes me look sickly white. I got born too early. I was smaller than a bag of sugar and I had to stay in hospital for weeks and weeks. I never really caught up with everyone else my age. Rochelle says I'm the runt of the litter.

The only garment I really like is my blue cardigan. It's magic because it stretches every time it's washed so it's grown with me the last two years.

My dad bought it for me. He took me out for the day, just him and me, and he saw I had goose pimples up and down my arms so he bought me my big blue cardie. I've worn it every day ever since. I've even worn it to school, though we're supposed to wear navy sweatshirts or jumpers. I got told off, but I insisted that blue's just like pale navy, so what was the problem? The teachers didn't bother to send a note home. They'd had enough arguments with my mum in the past when Martine and Jude and Rochelle were at our school.

I packed all my possessions into one of the cardboard boxes Jude had brought home from Tesco. There was my big book of fairy tales at the bottom. I didn't bother with the words, I just looked at lovely pictures of princesses with hair waving down to their knees, and made up my own stories. Then there were my notepads and fibre-tip colouring pens and my red gel pen that smelled of strawberries and my yellow gel pen that smelled of bananas. I had a Miss Kitty writing set too but I didn't really have anyone to write to. I had Martine's old one-eyed panda and Jude's monkey with the missing paw and Rochelle's old Barbies. I didn't play with them any more but I'd have felt mean if I'd chucked them out.

Rochelle had done *heaps* of chucking, but she still had two suitcases and three cardboard boxes brimming over with her bits.

Jude had even less clothes than me, and just one box containing her baseball bat and her biker boots and her videos and all her fantasy novels.

Martine was still refusing to pack. She wasn't speaking to Mum. She wasn't speaking to any of us, because we were all getting excited at the idea of a house with a garden now. Martine spent almost every second next door with Tony and his family. Mum got so mad at her she went and banged on Tony's mum's front door and

14

they had an argy-bargy right on the landing, Martine joining in too.

'Slagging off her own mother in front of everyone!' Mum wept afterwards. 'And me in my condition too.'

Jude and Rochelle and I had to do most of Mum's packing but we divided it up easily enough. Jude got all the heavy house stuff organized, Rochelle did Mum's clothes and make-up, and I did Mum's mystic paintings and her crystal ball and her tarot cards and astrology charts and *Every Woman's Easy Guide to Fortune Telling*.

I had to pack for little Sundance too. Mum had started buying enough little blue dungarees and sleeping suits and weeny fleeces for an entire nursery of baby boys. All brand new. Someone from the social had given her a black plastic rubbish bag full of old baby clothes but Mum wasn't grateful.

'It's a blooming insult, giving me this washed-out rubbish,' she said, tipping them out all over the carpet and stirring them disdainfully with her long pointed fingernails. 'For God's sake, look – sick stains!' she declared, stabbing at a faint white shadow on a little jacket. 'Right, this is all going in the bin where it belongs.'

She still hadn't decided on Sundance's nursery furniture. She'd gone off the Mothercare selection, and now wanted something more special.

'What, like Harrods?' said Jude.

She was being sarcastic but Mum took her seriously. 'I could check out their nursery stuff, certainly, but I think it might be a bit too traditional, you know? It would be great to get something specially designed, but that might be a bit too pricey.'

15

'Just a bit,' said Jude. She paused. 'Don't forget you've got to pay for the removal van.'

'Well, I was thinking of asking one of your dads for a bit of help.'

I sat up proudly. The only one of our dads Mum was still in touch with was *my* dad.

'I'll see if he can help us hire a van,' said Mum.

'Or loan us his hearse,' said Rochelle, cracking up laughing. Jude joined in. I stared at them, stony-faced.

'You shut up!' I said, so fiercely that they all took a step backwards, even Jude. 'Don't you dare laugh at my dad! I don't know why everyone thinks his job's so funny.'

'It's not funny, it's downright creepy,' said Rochelle, shuddering. 'It's a good thing you're not a little kid any more. Imagine holding his hand after he's been doing his day's embalming!'

'Yeah, actually, I had a bit of trouble with that aspect myself,' said Mum. 'I made him have a very long bath every time he came near me, but I still seemed to smell something weird on him.'

'He doesn't smell a bit!' I shouted, nearly crying.

'Of course he doesn't smell. *Mum's* the one that smells,' said Jude.

'Oi, you! I don't blooming well smell.'

'Yes, you do, of all those weird little oils,' said Jude.

'They're lovely, and they're doing me good too. I need neroli and lavender to calm me. No blooming wonder when I have to deal with you lot! Here, Dixie, take that scowl off your face. I didn't really mean it about your dad, darling, you know that. Come here.' Mum held her arms out and pulled me to sit on her lap, though her huge tummy meant I had to perch right at the end of her knees.

16

'Your dad's a very sweet guy,' Mum said softly. She divided my long hair until she found my ear. 'I think he's the best out of all my special guys,' she whispered.

Rochelle's got sharp ears. 'You always said *my* dad was your all-time favourite, Mum,' she said.

'All your dads were lovely guys,' Mum said. She sighed and settled back in her seat, patting her bump. She started chanting the dad story.

We all knew it backwards. She had soothed us to sleep telling us the tale when we were little. It was like our special bedtime story.

'First there was my lovely Dave, Martine's dad. We were childhood sweethearts. We first went out in Year Ten – imagine! We were so in love. Thought we knew it all too, as you do. I couldn't help being thrilled when I knew Martine was on the way, though I knew *my* mum would create. She always had a down on me, my mum, said I'd go to the bad. Dave did his best to stand by me, bless him. But how could he cope with a baby when he was still a kid himself?

'Then Jude's dad came along,' said Mum.

Jude blew a raspberry, but she listened all the same.

'Dean knew where he was going all right, and for a while he took care of me. He did his best to be a dad to Martine too. He could be so sweet and tender with us, he made my heart melt. But he could be a tricky guy too, especially if he was crossed. I loved him with all my heart but I knew I had to leave him when he started slapping me around.'

'Good riddance to him,' said Jude.

'Then there was *my* dad, Jordan,' said Rochelle. 'He was the best looking, wasn't he, Mum? I bet you'd have stayed with him for ever if he hadn't died.' She looked at me. 'Then *you* wouldn't be here today, Dixie. You wouldn't even exist.'

I knew she was just trying to wind me up, but I suddenly felt panicky. I looked down at myself, scared my arms and legs would start fading away as I turned into a ghost girl.

'Of course there was always going to be a Dixie,' said Mum. She waved her fingers in the air, squinting at five little lines on her palm. 'Read my hand! Four gorgeous girls – and one beautiful bouncing boy! It was always my destiny, darling. Maybe it's just as well I didn't sort out how it was all going to happen. It was so sad, losing my Jordan. You're right, Rochelle, he was so handsome my heart started hammering just at the sight of him. He was so talented too. He'd have been a real star in the music world if he'd only had the right breaks. It wasn't really his fault he got into the drug scene. It goes with the territory, right? Oh God, it was so awful awful awful when the police called me.' A tear slid down Mum's cheek. She always cried when she talked about Jordan.

Rochelle snuffled and puckered up like she was crying too. She always acts like losing her dad was the big tragedy of her life, but as he took his overdose when she was two years old I don't think she can even remember him.

Mum ran her hands through Rochelle's lovely long blonde hair and gave her a kiss on the cheek as if they were both still grieving.

I perched Bluebell on my finger and started grooming her feathers. Mum turned to me. I elbowed Rochelle out

18

the way. She pouted and pinged her fingers at Bluebell, making her fall off and land on her head.

'You pig,' I said, hitting out at her.

Rochelle dodged, laughing.

I cradled Bluebell, stroking her poor beak. 'You've bent it, Rochelle, look!'

'Oh dear, how will the poor little soul pick up all her birdseed now?' said Rochelle. 'Though I forgot, she doesn't *actually* eat, does she? And she clearly can't fly to save her life. Pretty duff sort of budgie, if you ask me.'

'And you're a pretty duff sort of girl to tease your poor sister so,' said Mum. 'Don't let her get to you, Dixie darling.'

'Tell me about *my* dad, Mum,' I said.

'That's just what I'm going to do, sweetheart. Dear Terry. I was so out of it, crying over Jordan, and Terry was so kind and talked to me for hours and hours, helping me sort everything out—'

'The oak coffin or the ash coffin or the deluxe mahogany lined with purple satin,' said Rochelle.

'Bog off, bad girlie,' said Mum. 'You can mock, but if it wasn't for Terry's sweetness I think I'd have gone right out of my mind. I was heading that way anyway, going a little bit bonkers every lonely evening—'

'And so you had a little bitty bonk with creepy old Terry,' said Rochelle.

'You're getting *way* too lippy, madam. Just you watch it. I might be eight months pregnant and the size of a flipping elephant but I can still sort you out, *no* problem,' said Mum. 'Terry is a lovely lovely guy and if only he didn't already have a family I'm sure we'd be together now. Though maybe I'm not destined to shack up with any of my guys for long. I figure it's us Diamond girls together – and we'll have to look to Junior here to look after us when we're all old ladies.'

'What about Junior's dad?' Jude said.

Mum sighed. 'I knew it was just going to be a brief encounter. He was so lovely and so artistic. Imagine, a painter! I wish he'd got to know you girls. I'd have loved him to do a portrait of all us Diamonds.'

'Why won't you tell us his name, Mum?' I said.

'Maybe she doesn't even know it,' Rochelle muttered.

'Honestly, Mum, why do you always have to get involved with all these guys?' said Jude.

'I'm not involved with anyone right now, Miss Priss. I must admit, I haven't been very lucky with my guys.'

'That's putting it mildly,' said Jude.

Mum pulled a face but refused to react. She rang my dad at his work to see if he could help us. It didn't sound as if he was pleased to hear from her. Mum kept sighing and pulling faces and going 'Yeah, yeah,' and 'Look, I don't ever bother you at home, darling, so quit nagging me. We do share a daughter. Do you want to have a little word with our Dixie?'

My throat went tight. I kept swallowing, trying to get enough spit into my mouth so I could speak. But I didn't have to. Mum nodded more.

'Sorry, Dixie, Dad sends his love and he'll be in touch very soon but he's up to his eyes in work right now,' said Mum.

'Up to his eyes in *corpses*?' said Rochelle.

Jude shoved her. Rochelle shoved back, squealing.

'Shut up, girls!' said Mum. 'No, no, listen, Terry, it'll

just take half a second – we're moving, we need a van. *Please*, darling, be a mate and help us.'

I waited, clutching Bluebell, just in case he changed his mind about having time to talk to me.

Mum put the phone down. She smiled reassuringly. 'There! All fixed!'

'Is Dad coming with a van?' I asked.

'No, he can't make it at the weekend, sweetie. It's difficult for him. I can understand. But he's got this mate, he'll get him to come. He might charge a bit, but it should just be peanuts. Dixie? Dad says he misses you a lot, sweetheart, and he told me to give you a big hug from him.'

I sloped off to my bedroom after Mum gave me the hug. My bed had all my stuff stacked on it so I curled up under Jude's duvet. She came in a few minutes after me.

'What are you doing in my bed? Hey, I sound like the three blooming bears!'

I kept my head in her pillow.

'Are you crying, Goldilocks?'

'No.'

'Fibber! Don't get my pillow all wet and snotty.'

'I've stopped now,' I said, sitting up and wiping my eyes on my cardigan sleeve.

'Were you crying just because you wanted to see your dad?' said Jude. 'You're daft, you. I don't *ever* see my dad and do I care?'

'Yeah, but your dad was nasty and hit Mum. And Martine. I expect he hit you too, even though you were just a baby.'

'I'd like to see him try now,' said Jude, punching the

air violently and making the bed bounce. 'I'd soon sort him out. Mum's much better off without him. She's much better off without *any* of them.'

'How come Mum can't see they're going to let her down when she looks into her crystal ball and reads the tarot and works out all her star charts?'

'Mum and her stupid crazes! Don't take it so seriously, Dixie. It's just a bit of glass and some old cards and some silly figures about stars. How can Mum possibly tell the future with that silly old rubbish?'

'Because she's psychic?'

'She's no more psychic than I am,' said Jude. She grabbed my hand. It was the one clutching Bluebell. She gave him a little stroke and then acted like he'd pecked her finger.

'Ouch! Keep your stunted little eagle under control, our Dixie! OK, let's see if I can read your palm. Ah! I see change on the horizon. Change of scenery – it says so in the stars. Or is it the planets? Here's your Mount of Mercury' – she tickled my palm – 'look how pronounced it is. It definitely features in the future. Ooh, what's this I see? Look at this wiggly line here. How significant is that!'

'What? What does it mean?' I knew Jude was only fooling around but she said it all in exactly Mum's tone of voice, making it sound so special, as if she really could read my palm.

'It means you're going to have fun on your new planet. See, the line squiggles around, just like a smile.' She traced the line for me.

I twisted my hand. 'But if you look *this* way it's a frown,' I said anxiously.

22

'Well, you'll have to keep your hand the right way up,' said Jude, tickling me. 'Now, what about this young budgie here? Hold out your wing, if you please.' Jude pretended to examine Bluebell's feather tips. 'Aha! Someone will be spreading their wings and flying off into the great blue yonder.'

'But then flying back to me?' I said.

'God, you're such a worryguts,' said Jude.

We heard Martine coming in. Mum said something, then Martine.

'I'm not bogging well going and that's that!' she yelled.

'Hm,' said Jude. 'It's easy predicting there's trouble ahead for *someone!*'

3

Martine still wasn't packed on Saturday, when we were moving. She stayed out all Friday night with Tony.

'She's simply making her point,' said Mum, wearily making us all tea and toast. She was still in her black silky nightie. It used to look slinky but now it was strained to the utmost, one of the seams starting to split.

'How come you're so cool about Martine staying out when you went absolutely bonkers when I came in at midnight that time?' said Jude, chewing toast.

'I knew Martine was safe next door, silly. You were skyrocketing around fighting with a lot of wild boys,' said Mum.

'What if Martine doesn't come back?' said Rochelle, licking honey off her toast with her pink pointy tongue.

'Quit messing around with your food like a toddler,' said Mum irritably. '*Eat* that toast. It's going to be a long day and we've got a hell of a lot to do.'

'If Martine stays with Tony's folks then I'll have our bedroom all to myself,' said Rochelle. She sounded hopeful.

Mum glared at her. 'Quit talking rubbish. Of course Martine's not staying at Tony's. Now come on, eat up, all of you. We've got to be all set and this tip cleared up by ten o'clock when the guy with the van comes for us.'

'My dad's pal,' I said proudly.

'I hope he's not another undertaker,' said Rochelle. 'He'll turn up wearing black and he'll carry our table on his shoulders very slowly, like it's a coffin.'

'My dad's not an undertaker, he's an embalmer,' I said.

'And he's not going to do all the humping around, apparently. He's got a bad back. It's our job to get the van loaded,' said Mum.

We stared at Mum in her tight black nightie. She looked like she'd explode if she lifted so much as a tray of teacups. Mum rubbed her stomach anxiously, pressing her lips together.

'Don't worry, Mum, we'll get it sorted,' said Jude.

'Yeah, Jude and I will carry all the furniture,' I said.

'You, pet!' said Mum, grabbing hold of me by the wrist.

I'm horribly small and scrawny for my age and I've got particularly stupid matchstick arms and legs. Jude's tried to teach me how to fight but I'm rubbish at it. I just duck if anyone attacks me. I've done a lot of ducking in the playground, especially after Jude went to secondary school. It didn't seem to make much difference when Rochelle left. She was sometimes the one doing the attacking.

'I'm not loading any stupid van. I'll break my nails and I've just got them perfect,' said Rochelle, waving her beautiful long pink nails, the thumbs decorated with little glass hearts.

'You're not loading the van, you're going to be doing

25

the scrubbing. Wear my Marigold gloves if you're fussed about your nails,' said Mum. 'No arguing, now! Let's all get cracking.'

Jude went out and rounded up some of her gang. She didn't like any of the boys but they all looked up to her. She soon had half the lads from North Block getting our furniture along the balcony, into the lift and out onto the courtyard.

I tucked Bluebell down the neck of my T-shirt, rolled up my cardie sleeves, and started heaving and shoving the cardboard boxes out the door. I tried lifting a couple, gasping and panting, but Mum made me stop.

'You're too little, Dixie. You'll do yourself an injury. Your womb will drop and you won't be able to have any babies.'

'Good!' I said. 'Look, I'll *shove* the boxes along the balcony, OK, Mum?'

'OK, pet, have a go. We're a bit strapped for time. I'll pack up all our Martine's gear seeing as her ladyship has failed to do it herself.'

'Shall we knock at Tony's door, Mum? Maybe she's overslept?'

'I'm not talking to his rubbish mother, not after the mouthful she gave me. I wouldn't graze my knuckles on her front door. No, Martine will just have to put in her appearance when she's good and ready.'

'But what if she doesn't?'

'I don't think she will,' Rochelle said, still hoping. 'Oh bum, I've got my jeans all gungy kneeling on the kitchen floor. My *best* jeans!'

'Why wear your best jeans when we're moving? What are you *like*, Rochelle?' Mum fussed, spilling Martine's clothes on her bed and then rolling them up in her duvet.

'I didn't know I was going to be doing the bogging scrubbing. It's not fair, you always give me the worst jobs, Mum. How come Martine gets out of doing her fair share? She made just as much a mess so she should be scrubbing too, even though she's maybe not coming with us.'

'There's no blooming maybe, I keep telling you!' Mum said fiercely, emptying Martine's drawers into a big laundry bag. She shook the drawer vigorously, so that little rolled-up socks and wispy thongs and snaky tights bounced all over the carpet. 'Of course she's coming. She lives with us. She's family.'

We heard footsteps along the balcony and then a tap at the front door.

'There she is!' said Mum triumphantly.

It wasn't Martine. It was a small skinny guy with a bad haircut and round glasses. They didn't sit comfortably so he had to wrinkle his nose and hitch them up every few seconds.

'Hi,' he said, glancing at Mum's stomach anxiously. 'I'm Terry's mate.'

'Oh yeah, great. You're the guy with the van,' said Mum.

'I'm Dixie,' I said, pushing past her. 'You're my dad's best pal, aren't you?'

'Well, I know Terry, yes, through work.'

'I *said* he'd be an undertaker,' Rochelle whispered, giggling behind me.

'No, no, I've got this florist's business. Hence the van.' He pointed over the balcony way down to a white van with FREDA'S FLOWERS in fancy gold lettering.

27

'Oh, I see. You're Freda, are you?' said Mum.

We all sniggered. He sighed. It was obviously a joke he'd got sick and tired of long ago.

'Freda was my mum. It was her business. Now she's gone, I run it. I'm . . .' He hesitated for a second. 'I'm Bruce.'

'Hello, Bruce. I'm Sue Diamond and these are all my girls. Well, shall we get cracking?'

Bruce looked anxious. 'Terry did tell you I can't lift anything, didn't he? I mean, I'd like to help, seeing as you're . . .' He gestured tactfully.

'Yeah, no worries, mate, we've got everything under control,' said Mum. She tucked her hand through his arm like they were great pals already. 'You're a sweetheart to help us out.'

'Well, it's just a business deal,' Bruce said nervously. 'I drive you there with all your stuff for fifty quid, right? I need to be back at the shop this afternoon though. I'm short-staffed, and there might be deliveries – bouquets and that.'

'Sure, sure, we'll be all moved into our dream house by then,' said Mum. 'So let's get cracking, girls, and get the last of the stuff downstairs.' She gave Bruce's arm a squeeze. 'How about you carrying these clothes, darling?'

'But I've done my back in, Mrs Diamond, like I said.'

'Call me Sue, silly. I've never been a Mrs in my life, I'm my own woman. I know you've got a bad back, mate. So have I, as a matter of fact. You try having a big bruiser of a baby boy leaning up close and personal against your spine! I'm not asking you to shift a blooming wardrobe, just a few little flimsy clothes that hang inside it. You can do that, can't you, Bruce?'

28

Bruce saw he didn't have any choice. He let Mum thrust the duvet containing all Martine's clothes into his arms.

'I'll help you carry some,' I said, seeing as he was still sort of my dad's friend.

'No, Dixie, you start rolling up the rugs. Look at that fluff! Rochelle, you were meant to sweep under them, you dodo. Jude, you get all your boy pals loading our stuff into the van, OK?' Mum said, giving us all little pokes as she organized us.

She prodded Bruce too and so he started plodding along the balcony, Martine's clothes flapping over his arms.

Then there was a bang of a door, and a lot of shouting. Bruce shuffled back again, looking bewildered. Martine was yelling at him.

'Mum? What's going on? What's this creep doing with all my clothes?' she shouted.

'He's not a creep, he's my dad's friend!' I said indignantly.

'Yes, don't you dare come marching in here, yelling and screaming and showing us all up, madam,' said Mum, folding her arms above her stomach.

'I'm yelling because you're getting rid of all my clothes!' said Martine. She had dark circles under her eyes and her hair was sticking up all over the place, like she'd tossed and turned all night. 'I know you're mad at me, Mum, but I never thought you'd throw all my clothes out!' She was breathing heavily as if she might start crying any minute.

Mum was working herself up too, her face blotchy with rage. 'What do you think I'm doing, sending them all off to Oxfam?' she shouted.

'Well, that's what it looks like, doesn't it?' said Martine. 'Look, even my leather jacket!' She plucked it from Bruce's arms, starting an avalanche of clothes all over the hall. Bruce shrank back against the wall, bracing himself for another onslaught.

'What do you want me to do?' he asked helplessly.

'You pick up all those clothes and take them down to the van,' Mum snapped, as if he'd dropped them deliberately.

Bruce gathered up the clothes and sloped off, side-stepping Martine as she made a half-hearted grab at them.

'Stop it, Martine!' said Mum.

'You stop it, Mum. There's no point putting all my stuff in the van. I'm not coming. Can't you get that into your head? I'm staying with Tony, no matter what. I love him.'

Mum raised her hand. I was sure she was going to slap her. Martine thought so too and tried to dodge. But Mum's hand curved gently round Martine's flushed cheek, cupping her chin.

'Martine, pet, can't you learn by my mistakes? I know you love Tony – but it won't last.'

'It will, it will! We're going to love each other for ever.' Martine brushed Mum's hand away. Mum's arm swung sadly, her fingers still outstretched. She took a deep breath.

'If you're going to love each other for ever then can't you give me a month or two? I need you to help settle us into the new place. I can't manage just now, not with the baby making me so bulky. I can't lift or carry or stretch. See what I'm like,' said Mum, acting it out.

'We'll help you, Mum,' I said.

30

'Oh, Dixie! You're too little, like I said.' Mum lowered her voice. 'And Jude's not girly enough and Rochelle's too scatty.' She looked deep into Martine's eyes. 'I need you, darling. You're my girl, my eldest. You and me together, Martine, making it work. You don't have to stay once your baby brother's born and I can run around all over the shop. Help me. Please. I can't make it work, not without you.' Tears started dripping down Mum's cheeks. She didn't blink or try to wipe them away. She stared steadily at Martine.

Martine suddenly started crying too. 'Oh Mum,' she said. She threw her arms round Mum's neck. 'All right, I'll come.'

'I knew you would,' said Mum, hugging her tight.

'Just till the baby's born.'

'Well, give me a week or two after to recover. I'm not getting any younger, you know. I can't snap straight back into action the way I did when I had you, darling. Still, they say boys are easier. I hope the little whatsit sleeps soundly. I don't fancy all that two-o'clock-in-the-morning feeding caper.'

'Well *I'm* not doing it!' said Martine, but she clung onto Mum, nuzzling her head against her neck as if she was still a baby herself.

'My big girlie,' Mum said softly, running her fingers through Martine's tufty hair.

'Typical!' said Rochelle, pushing past to wave her grubby mop over the balcony. 'I do all the hard work, scrubbing away like stupid Cinderella, ruining my only decent jeans in the process, and *she* gets all this fussing. How come manky old Martine's your favourite, Mum?'

'You're *all* my favourite Diamond girls,' said Mum.

'Little sparkling gems, the lot of you – especially the pretty one with the Marigold gloves.'

Rochelle peeled off her pink rubber gloves and flapped their flabby fingers at Mum. Mum grabbed one for herself and they had a silly Marigold glove slap-and-flap fight.

Bruce came back empty-armed and stepped warily round them, shaking his head. 'I'm not sure I like all those young lads getting in and out my van,' he said. 'I know some are helping load your stuff but there's others just generally mucking about. One of them was fiddling with the steering wheel and when I ticked him off he gave me a mouthful you'd never believe.'

'Oh, I'd believe it all right,' said Mum. 'Don't you worry, Bruce, mate, just tell our Jude and she'll soon sort them out for you. We're nearly done anyway. I can't wait to get out of this dump and start out in our lovely new house, eh, girls?'

Martine didn't look like she agreed one little bit. She went to tell Tony she was coming with us after all. He came down to see us off when the van was fully packed. He didn't say a word to any of us, but he took Martine in his arms and gave her a really passionate twirly-tongue kiss.

Mum tutted but didn't try to stop them. All Jude's gang hooted and catcalled, while Jude herself mimed being sick. Rochelle looked envious. I wasn't sure what I felt. I rather wanted someone to love me lots, but I thought it would feel very wet and squirmy kissing like that. I decided I preferred budgies to boyfriends as they just gave you neat dry pecks of affection.

The biggest boy in Jude's gang suddenly caught hold of her by the wrist and started kissing *her*. Jude wasn't having any of it. She gave him such a shove he staggered backwards onto his bottom. Jude rubbed her lips with the back of her hand, shuddering, like she was removing slug-slime. All the other boys howled.

Rochelle sidled up to them, tossing her fair curls over her shoulder. She sucked her mouth into a little pink pout to show that *she* wouldn't mind a kiss. The boys jostled around her, some of them making kissy-kissy noises, but they were just teasing her. Rochelle flounced into the van.

'Honestly, what creeps,' she said. 'I don't know why you hang round with that crowd, Jude.'

'I don't hang round them. They hang round me,' said Jude.

'Yeah, well, say goodbye to your little gang,' said Mum. 'We're off now. Put Tony down, Martine, and get in the van. Let's get going.'

Bruce steered the van very slowly round all the blocks while we did our best to steady all the stuff in the back. Mum wound down a window.

'Bye, boring old Bletchworth!' she shouted at the top of her voice.

People turned and stared. Some of the women shook their heads and tutted. Mum blew raspberries at them all. Lots of the men wolf-whistled. Even the decorator guys painting the windowsills on South Block bent down from their cradles and waved. Their little gang had been painting the whole Bletchworth Estate for months. All the girls were crazy about the youngest guy, who was dark with a cheeky grin. He went out with a different girl every night and he was already a dad, even though he was only seventeen.

He seemed to have taken a shine to our Martine because he called out, 'Bye, gorgeous, nice knowing you!' He waved so wildly he dropped his paintbrush and it landed with a thump on the top of Bruce's van.

'Blooming heck! What an idiot! I hope he hasn't made a dent in my van,' said Bruce. 'Let's get out of here before he starts hurling his paint pots too.'

Mum was laughing but she was crying too.

'Are you sad, Mum? Don't you want to go now?'

'I'm fine, Dixie. Of course I want to go. This is the start of our brand-new life. Let's get that wheel of fortune whirling!'

4

'Are we nearly there yet?' I said.

'For God's sake, Dixie, we've only been driving ten minutes!' said Mum.

'I think I'm starting to feel sick,' I said.

'Breathe deeply and look straight ahead,' said Bruce. 'I'll buy you some barley sugar at the next service station.'

'Thank you, Uncle Bruce.'

'I'm not your uncle, dear.'

Still, he acted like an uncle, buying us all sweets when he stopped for petrol. I still felt sick. It didn't help that I was squashed up the wrong way, but I was so wedged in with boxes I couldn't turn round. Martine was practically sitting on top of me, texting Tony non-stop on her mobile. Jude and Rochelle were fighting over who had more room, fiercely shoving each other. I sometimes got in the way of their shoves. I clutched Bluebell and pretended we were flying right out of the window, soaring straight into the sky, up to our own silent, sisterless planet.

It seemed a very long way to the Planet Estate. Mum started to get as bored as us girls.

'I'm starving,' she said.

'Have a barley sugar,' said Bruce, offering her the packet.

'I'm eating for two, mate. I need more than a blooming barley sugar. Come on, let's stop for a snack. We could have an early lunch, give us a bit of energy for all the unpacking.'

She made Bruce stop at the next service station. We wandered round and round the food court in a daze. There was so much to choose from, not just the same old stuff you get down the chippy or the Chinese.

Martine said first of all that she was too miserable to eat. Then she said she'd just have a salad. And maybe a piece of cold chicken. And a packet of crisps. And some fruit. And maybe a KitKat and a coffee.

Jude had a large plateful of spaghetti bolognese.

Rochelle had a Cornetto and a cream doughnut and a Mars bar.

I had prawn sandwiches. I didn't like the sandwich part but I enjoyed picking out the little pink prawns and making them swim across my plate. Then I had a bowl of strawberries and whipped cream. I spent ages spooning on the cream so that each red strawberry mountain had its own cap of creamy snow.

Mum had macaroni cheese for the baby's benefit and a big bowl of chips for herself. She tried to get Bruce to have chips too and a big mixed grill. 'I like to see a man eat a proper plateful,' she said. Bruce said he could only stomach tea and toast mid morning. He paid for it hurriedly, counting it out in coins.

Mum nudged up close with her tray, calling for us all to come over quick. It looked like she was hoping Bruce might pay for our lunch too. Bruce looked terrified and made for a table so quickly he bumped his tray and spilled half his tea over his buttered toast. Mum had to pay. The bill came to £36.99.

'Rubbish!' said Mum. She said a worse word, actually.

The lady at the till blinked at her. 'Language!' she said.

'Yeah, well, the Queen herself would start effing and blinding at this sort of rip-off,' said Mum. 'You add that up again. You must have added at least a tenner.'

'Mum!' Martine hissed. 'You're showing us up!'

'We could put some stuff back,' I suggested, though I'd already winkled a couple of prawns out of my sandwich and eaten the biggest strawberry.

'I've only got a snack – unlike *some* people,' said Rochelle, nudging Jude.

'I bet my spag bol cost less than all your rubbish,' said Jude, nudging her back.

'Shut up, girls. No, you're not putting anything back. OK OK, we'll pay for our food, but let's hope you've got gold knives and forks to eat it with,' said Mum, fishing two twenties out of her purse.

She didn't have much money left, yet she still had to pay Bruce for driving us. I hoped the Planet Estate would have a good chippy because that's what we'd be eating all week.

Bruce hunched up small when we all sat down with him, holding his plate of soggy toast as if we were about to snatch it away from him. Mum tried to chat to him to show she had no hard feelings over him not forking out for our meal, but he kept shrugging and shaking his

37

head. He kept peering round to see if people were looking at us. Maybe he was embarrassed to be seen out with us in case people thought he was our dad.

'How's your toast, Uncle Bruce?' I asked, squeezing up beside him.

'It's OK. It's just toast. I'm not your uncle, I said.'

'Do you know any of my real uncles? Or aunties? Or maybe my gran and grandad?' I asked, leaning up so close I could whisper in his ear. I didn't want Mum to hear me. She always said we didn't need any other family. She said we were a fine family all by ourselves, the Diamond girls.

So how come she was so desperate for this baby *boy*?

'I don't know your dad's folks, Trixie. I don't even know your dad that well. We're just work mates, really. I deliver the wreaths.'

'So you've never been to his house?'

'Well, a couple of times. Socializing. He's always having people round, your dad.'

'He's never had *me* round,' I said. 'Tell me what his place is like, Uncle Bruce, please!'

'Well, it's just . . . just a house. It's modern, quite comfy. Maybe a bit too full of satin cushions and ruffled curtains, but then I'm a bloke, so I wouldn't really go for anything too frilly and feminine.'

'Why does my dad want frilly stuff then?'

'It's Stella's taste, dear.'

'Who?'

'You know. His wife,' said Bruce, buttering his second slice of toast. 'She's very girly, like. And his girls are all fluffy curls and lipstick too. Even the baby's a curlyknob, all dainty and dimples.'

I felt as if he'd stabbed me straight in the ribs with his knife. I put my prawn sandwich down. I tore at the crusts, turning them into breadcrumbs. I remembered the fairy story of Hansel and Gretel and how they were abandoned in a forest because their mum and dad didn't want them. They left a trail of breadcrumbs so they could find their way back. I didn't get that. Why would they want to go back to such horrible parents? I decided I'd stay in the forest. I wouldn't go near that gingerbread cottage and get caught by the wicked witch. I wouldn't even have a lick of her candy-cane door knocker. I'd clear off and make my own cottage. Bluebell would live with me. I'd have a trapeze in my garden and she'd have her perch and we'd swing in unison and turn somersaults just like a circus act.

'Dixie! Stop daydreaming. You look so gormless with your mouth hanging open. Do you have to mangle your food like that? Especially when that sandwich cost me a fortune! Pull yourself together! Bruce is talking to you.'

I knew Bruce was talking. I'd been trying to get him to tell me stuff about my dad all morning but now he'd started I didn't want to hear. I knew my dad had a wife and two other daughters but I didn't want to think about them. I hadn't known he had a new baby. I didn't want to think about her. It was the one thing I'd always counted on. *I* was his baby.

I'd been a dreadful baby. Mum and Martine and Jude and Rochelle had told me often enough. I'd been premature, like a little skinned rabbit, all purple and shrieking my head off. I went on shrieking for months and months, wanting to be fed every three hours, night and day.

'Tiny little thing, but you had the lungs of a bull-moose,' said Mum. 'God, you didn't half bellow! And then you were forever *ill* – jaundice and eczema and croup. I'd walk you up and down, up and down, and you'd yell and wheeze and scratch and scream until I very nearly chucked you out the window.'

It was no wonder my dad never wanted to see much of me.

I muttered something about going to the toilet and mooched off while Bruce was in mid-sentence. I was sick of hearing about babies.

I sat in the toilets a long time, reading all the rude rhymes on the door. I stroked Bluebell on my lap and pretended she was flying up above every cubicle, peeking at everyone peeing. I heard Mum and the girls come in, calling for me. I kept quiet and clutched Bluebell by the beak.

I waited until Mum's voice got high and panicky and then I pulled the chain and sauntered out. I tried to look surprised when Mum rushed at me.

'There you are! Oh dear lord, we've been calling till we're hoarse. I was about to phone the police. I thought someone must have whipped you away with them.' Mum hugged me hard. 'Didn't you hear me calling, Dixie?'

'Course she heard. She was just winding us all up,' said Rochelle, tossing her hair.

'I *didn't* hear,' I said. Well, I'd tried hard not to.

'So what were you doing all this time?'

'I had a funny tummy,' I said. This wasn't exactly a lie. My tummy had screwed itself up into a knot the moment Bruce mentioned my dad's baby.

'There! I bet it was that prawn sandwich,' said Mum.

'It wouldn't affect her immediately,' said Martine, putting blusher on her pale cheeks. 'God, I look such a sight. I'm scared Tony's going to go off me. What if he clicks with some other girl while I'm away?'

'Oh shut it, Martine,' said Jude. 'What if *you* click with some other guy?'

'Tony's my one and only,' said Martine. She said it seriously but it sounded so silly we all laughed, and even Martine sniggered a little.

'*Ton-eee's my one and oh-oh-onleee,*' Rochelle sang, camping it up.

'You are so *wet*, Martine,' said Jude.

'So are you – now!' said Martine. She flipped her hand under the running tap and squirted Jude in the face.

They started having a grand water fight until Mum bashed them with her handbag.

'For God's sake, girls, stop acting like little kids. Look at you, you're soaked! Come on, let's get going. Bruce will be wondering what the hell has happened to us.'

He was prowling nervously up and down outside the Ladies. He looked astonished to see Martine and Jude dripping wet but didn't bother to pass comment. He did edge up to me, though.

'You all right, Trix— Dixie?' He fidgeted. 'Your mum pointed out I wasn't being tactful, going on about your dad's family. I didn't mean any harm. I thought you *wanted* me to tell you stuff about him. I didn't mean for you to get upset.'

'I'm fine, I'm fine,' I said. I fiddled around up my cardigan sleeve, feeling for Bluebell.

'You looking for a hankie?' asked Bruce.

I shook my head. I remembered I'd stuffed Bluebell

down my T-shirt. I felt for her, pretending I had an itch. She slipped through my fingers and swallow-dived to the floor. I picked her up quickly, blushing.

'Is that a budgie?' said Bruce. 'I had a budgie when I was a little boy.'

'A real one?'

'Yes, our Sammy. We used to let him out of his cage and he'd perch right on the top of my head, singing away. He could do all sorts of tricks.'

'I'm going to have a real budgie but I won't keep it in a cage because I think that's cruel. I'm going to train it like a hawk so it flies around wherever it wants but comes when I whistle to it.'

'Oh yes? I think you might have to do quite a lot of whistling,' said Bruce. He ruffled my hair. 'I'll tell your dad you're a really cute kid when I see him.'

'Did he ask how I was then?'

I saw his eyes flickering behind his glasses.

'Yes, he did. That's right, and he also asked me to tell him exactly what you look like now.'

'Oh!' I fiddled with my hair, and turned over the grubby cuffs of my cardigan. 'I look a mess.'

'No you don't. I'll tell him you look little, but very pretty.'

I stared up at Bruce. 'I think maybe you need new glasses!' I said.

Bruce smiled at me. He had rather goofy teeth and they showed a lot when he smiled. He remembered and put his hand over his mouth to hide them.

'I'm glad you and my dad are mates,' I said.

He didn't point out they weren't mates this time. He nodded at me and gave me a little pat on the shoulder.

42

Mum was busy rounding up the girls. Martine was on the phone again, Jude was looking at action videos in the shop and Rochelle was flicking through magazines.

'Put that back, Rochelle, I'm not buying it. I don't care whose pin-up they've got inside. I've just spent a small fortune on a meal. We've got a whole house to fix up now.'

'How do you mean, fix up?' said Jude.

'Well, they said it might need a coat of paint, a little bit of work here and there. Nothing major. We could give a painting party, all hands on deck, eh?'

Mum was looking at Bruce's hands in particular. His fingers became fists.

'It's council, isn't it? They'll get it painted for you,' he said.

'Oh bless! Yeah, if you're prepared to wait ten years. I'm having a baby, sweetheart, and my little boy needs a nice new blue nursery. And all my girls want lovely bright bedrooms too, don't you, darlings?'

'Count me out, Mum. You know I'm just here till the baby's born,' Martine said.

'You sound like a stuck CD. I've got the message,' said Mum. 'But wait till you see the house, Martine, you might just be tempted to stay. It's going to be lovely, you'll see. I can just picture it. The Planet Estate's practically out in the country. We can get a buggy with really big bouncy wheels and take the baby for long country walks, get some roses in his little cheeks—'

'And there's a garden, isn't there, Mum?' I said.

'We'll make it a lovely garden. Maybe grow roses. And what's that creeper stuff that smells good? Honeysuckle! We'll drape it all round the front door.

43

Maybe we could have a water feature like Charlie with the chest, though that might be a bit dodgy when the baby starts to walk.'

We talked houses and gardens for ages in the van. We didn't seem to be getting near any countryside. We stayed stuck on grim motorways for a long time and then we branched off into a bleak grey town of ugly square buildings and torn-down posters and scribbled-over walls. There were six enormous concrete tower blocks on the horizon.

'God, what a dump!' Mum muttered.

Bruce glanced at her. I didn't like his expression.

We drove on down smaller streets of terraced houses and corner shops with iron shutters. Black plastic rubbish bags were strewn all over the pavements, many of them leaking.

I hunched down to see the six tower blocks. They were getting nearer. I knew what their names were: Mercury, Mars, Venus, Neptune, Jupiter and Saturn.

Jude was sitting very still too, craning her neck, a look of horror on her face. Martine stopped texting Tony and stared too, her finger blindly stabbing the air. Rochelle stopped singing, though her mouth stayed open. We didn't say a word, hoping we were wrong.

Mum prattled on, chatting to us, chatting to Bruce, even chatting to the baby. 'Who's my gorgeous boy, then? Stop that kicking now and listen to Mummy. Who's going to be brought up in a lovely new house then, with his own blue bedroom and his own beautiful big garden? You can run about all you please, my little darling, play footie to your heart's content. You're going to live happily ever after, my little Diamond boy.'

Bruce turned down a street of sad falling-down houses, half of them boarded up. Brambles rioted in the gardens. We all saw the street sign. Mercury Street.

5

Thirty Mercury Street had rude words spray-painted all over the front door and the brickwork. Two of the upstairs windows were broken and boarded up with cardboard. Water dripped forlornly from the toilet overflow, staining the grey-pebbledash underneath. The front garden was a rubbish tip of McDonald's boxes, Kentucky Fried Chicken cartons and empty beercans. There were no flowers, no grass, just knee-high dandelions.

Bruce switched off the ignition. We sat motionless inside the van. No one said a word. Then Mum shook her head.

'This *can't* be it,' she said. She opened the van door and heaved herself out. She blinked at the house, shaking her head. 'It isn't our house,' she said, her hands clasped protectively round the baby.

'Yes it is, Mum. Number thirty. And this is Mercury – it said so back there,' said Jude, jumping out and standing beside Mum. She looked round warily. There didn't seem to be anyone about but it wasn't the sort of place where you left things to chance.

I wriggled out beside them and held onto Jude's hand. She didn't try to swat me away.

'I'm not getting out. It's way too scary,' said Rochelle.

'I can't believe it, Mum,' said Martine. 'You've messed up my entire life and got rid of our lovely flat for *this* dump?'

'It's *not* our house! I saw it. The girl down the council showed me photos on her computer, I swear she did. It was lovely, all prettily painted with flowers in the garden. The houses weren't wrecks, they all looked brand new,' Mum said wildly, whirling round and round as if she might suddenly spot the real Mercury houses on the horizon.

'It *was* brand new – once,' Martine said. 'She obviously showed you photos from years and years ago, when the estate was newly built. Why didn't you *realize* that? If the houses were really that special there'd be a waiting list, wouldn't there? But no one else would ever be mad enough in a million years to put their names down for this dump.'

'Let's all get back in the van and go *home*,' said Rochelle.

'We can't,' said Mum. 'It's allocated already. *This* is our home.' She stared at it and started crying. 'Oh my God, what have I done?'

'You're so stupid, Mum. You don't ever think,' said Martine.

'Shut up,' said Jude. She put her arm round Mum. 'Don't cry. It's not good for the baby. It's OK. It's maybe not so bad inside. Let's go and look.'

Mum had the keys in an envelope, but you didn't really need them. It wasn't worth locking 30 Mercury Street.

All self-respecting thieves would give it a wide berth. It smelled damp and stale and musty. I nuzzled my nose into my cardigan sleeve.

The stained carpet had been half ripped up and lay curled over on itself in the middle of the living room. Someone had used it as a picnic bench. There were screwed-up fish and chip papers and empty lager cans littered all round it. The walls were all scribbled over. Some giant graffiti artists had even left their tag marks right across the ceiling.

We went into the kitchen. Someone had been sick in the sink.

'Yuck!' Rochelle squealed. 'Quick, let's get *out* of here. We can't stay here, we simply *can't*.'

'Let's see the bedrooms,' Martine said grimly.

We trooped up the stairs, Jude taking Mum by the arm and leading her, like she'd suddenly become an old lady. There was one big bedroom, two smaller rooms and a tiny cupboard room.

'Which do you want, Rochelle?' Jude asked.

'I don't care,' said Rochelle tearfully. 'They're all rubbish. I'm not stopping here.'

'Well, *I'm* only here till the baby comes. I did say so, all along,' said Martine.

Mum looked dazed. 'How can I have a baby here?' she said. 'How can I look after you girls in a place like this? How can I? How?'

No one knew how to answer her. We trailed downstairs again, where Bruce was waiting in the living room, glancing anxiously out of the window at his van.

'I'd better keep an eye on it,' he said. 'Shall we start unloading now?'

'I can't put our stuff in this house. It's filthy!' said Mum.

'Well, I can't keep it in the van, Sue,' said Bruce. 'I'm sorry, but I've got to get back sharpish. I thought this was going to be a simple moving job, cash in hand, not all day with lots of humping furniture around.'

He was hinting to Mum he wanted his money now, plus a tip for his trouble, but she wasn't connecting with him. She was looking at the letter in the key envelope and then trying to make a call on her mobile.

'Oh Gawd, I haven't topped it up. Martine, here, lend us yours.'

'But I want to phone Tony.'

'Just hand me the blessed phone for two minutes, will you? I'm sick of you moaning on that mobile, telling tales on me to your wretched Tony. You're acting like I've done this on *purpose*. I wasn't to know.'

'You should have found out first. You're the mother. Though a fat lot of use you are as a mother,' said Martine, shoving her mobile in Mum's hand.

'Shut it, Martine, I'm telling you,' said Jude.

'I'm trying my best,' said Mum, sniffing. She dialled the number and then breathed out in an angry hiss. 'Typical! They've put me on hold and they're playing "We All Live in a Yellow Submarine". It has to be some sick joke, right? We want to know where *we're* going to live. Because it ain't *here*. Don't worry, kids. We'll get this sorted soon.'

Mum had her head up, her chin jutting, her chest thrust out, her huge belly heaving. For a moment she looked like a comic book super-hero, able to snap her fingers and make our beautiful house appear as if by

49

magic. But then I blinked and she was just my mum again, starting to bite her nails, her face screwed up with worry. It wasn't going to happen.

Mum did her best. When she finally got through to the Housing Department she ranted, she raved, she wept, she pleaded. She said she had four children and was about to give birth to her fifth any minute. It didn't make any difference.

Mum stabbed the off button on Martine's mobile so hard she hurt her finger and had to nurse it in her armpit. 'Pigs! Rotten useless unfeeling pigs!' she said, rocking with the pain. 'They say they sent a team to clear up the house once I'd signed for it and they can't help it if someone's broken in and mucked it up meanwhile.'

'Can't they give us another house, Mum?' said Rochelle.

'They say they've hardly got any now, they've all been sold off. It's this stinking dump or one of them huge hostels full of refugees,' said Mum. 'They won't offer me anything decent because I signed for this tenancy.'

'Yes, well, you were mad to sign, weren't you?' said Martine relentlessly.

'I know. OK? You're right. Do you think I feel good about it?' said Mum. 'I feel bloody terrible.' She collapsed onto the rolled-up carpet and started crying, her head in her hands. We stood round her in a ring, watching helplessly. Bruce stood in the doorway, holding his van keys.

'Don't upset yourself,' he mumbled.

Mum cried harder.

'You'll make yourself ill,' Bruce said, trying to sound firmer. 'And you've got to get organized.'

It was clear Mum was past organization now.

'Well, *someone*'s got to sort things out,' said Bruce. He looked at Martine, because she's the eldest.

'Don't look at me,' she said furiously.

Bruce's eyes swivelled to Jude. She glared at him and went to sit beside Mum on the carpet. She put her arm round her.

Bruce looked at Rochelle. She was in tears too.

'This is a horrible horrible horrible house and I hate it. I want to go *home*,' she wept.

I was the only one left. Bruce looked at me. He shook his head and sighed. He took a deep breath. 'OK. Here's what we'll do,' he said. 'You two little girls, Rosanne and Dixie, try to get the house cleared up a bit. You two big girls help me unload the van. I can't do too much. If I do my back in again there'll be hell to pay.'

'I'm not a little girl! I'm *Rochelle*, not Rosanne! I'm not cleaning! I did all the rotten cleaning back home. And this is disgusting. I'm not touching *sick*!'

'OK, OK, I'll do the sick in the sink,' said Bruce, starting to roll his sleeves up. 'Then we'll *have* to get the van unloaded. I've got to get back. I'm very very late as it is. If you lot don't co-operate I'll just have to drive off with all your stuff still on board. I don't want to, but you're leaving me no option. You're not being *fair*.'

'No, we're not,' I said. 'I'll help, Uncle Bruce.'

'I don't think a little titch like you can hump furniture, sweetheart,' said Bruce, but he nodded at me gratefully.

'Little *squirt*,' said Rochelle rudely. She felt in her shoulder bag, found her pink Marigolds and threw them at me. 'Here you are then if you're so eager to get cleaning. *I'm* not having some weirdo guy telling *me* what to do.'

51

Her aim wasn't good. One of the gloves landed on Mum's head, sticking to her long black hair like a giant water lily. Mum swatted it away wearily. She wiped her eyes with the back of her hand and smeared mascara across her cheeks.

'Oh bum. I must look a right sight. Quit showing off, Rochelle. Take no notice, Bruce, she's always been a stroppy little cow. Now come on, girls, chop-chop, do like Bruce says.' She smiled up at him, all tears and smudges. 'Thank you, sweetheart, you're a star. I *knew* you'd help us.'

Bruce sighed. He threw his van keys to Jude. 'You make a start with the furniture then. You look like you're the strong girl of the family.'

It was exactly the right thing to say to Jude. She jumped to it. Bruce thrust his fingers into the rubber gloves and strode resolutely to the kitchen.

We watched Jude opening the van doors and reaching in for the first of the boxes. She staggered a little as she hauled it to the pavement.

'She'll hurt herself. I'll help her,' said Mum, trying to get up.

'Oh for God's sake, you can't shift huge boxes in your condition. I'll have to do it,' Martine said, and she stomped out to help Jude.

'Well, I'm not doing *anything*,' said Rochelle.

'Yes, you are, darling. You're going to ferret in the van for the carrier with the cleaning stuff because all them sinks and toilets are going to need a lot of bleach. *I'm* going to do that. *You're* going to be chief clothes girl, getting all our gear unpacked out of all the boxes and bags.'

Rochelle huffed and puffed but did as she was told.

'What can *I* do, Mum?' I asked.

'You can help me up for a start, Dixie. I'm stuck here like Little Miss Muffet on her blooming tuffet,' said Mum.

I held her hands and pulled hard. Mum staggered to her feet. She straightened up slowly, rubbing her tummy.

'Phew! I'll be glad when he's born. Three weeks to go! Still, I'm glad it's all plain sailing this time. Not like when I had you, little darling. You came two months early and scared me silly.'

'Does it hurt horribly when you have a baby?'

'Well, it's no picnic,' said Mum.

'Worse than being punched?'

'It's different.' Mum reached out with her fingers and gently poked the corners of my mouth. 'Hey! Where's my smiley babe? Don't worry so, I'll be fine. Your little brother will pop out no problem. Boys are meant to be much easier than girls.' Mum rubbed her face. 'Am I still all mascara smudges?'

'A bit. Here.' I licked my finger and rubbed hard. 'It was scary when you cried like that, Mum.'

'Oh tosh. I wasn't *really* crying. I was just putting it on so old Bruce would stop fussing and fretting and make himself useful,' said Mum, giving me a hug.

'Oh yeah. I knew that really,' I fibbed.

'No, you didn't! You'll believe anything, my baby girl.' Mum held onto me, rocking me. 'I know I'm having my baby boy but you're still my baby girl, Dixie.'

'Come off it, Mum. I'm not a baby any more.'

'Yes you are! You'll be my baby when you're a little old lady of eighty and I'm an ancient old bag of a hundred and goodness knows what. OK! Let's get cracking. Maybe I can't hump furniture but I can clean.'

53

'I'll clean too, Mum. Not the sick though.'

'Well, old Bruce seems to be tackling that,' said Mum, cocking her head and listening to running water in the kitchen. 'I knew he'd turn up trumps.'

'He's got to get back though. Urgent.'

'I bet I can twist him round my little finger. You wait and see, little Dix.' Mum rubbed her tummy as if she was Aladdin and it was her magic lamp. 'He's a gentleman, our Bruce. He's not going to abandon a pregnant lady.'

She suddenly doubled up, her face contorted.

'Mum?' I said. '*Mum!*'

Mum looked up and burst out laughing. 'Fooled you! And I'll fool Bruce too.'

'Oh Mum, you are *bad!*' I pretended to smack her.

Mum caught hold of me and gave me a big hug. 'Bless your dad for finding him. He never lets me down.'

I gave Mum a big hug back.

'You're always there for me too, babe. You and all my girls. Diamond girls stick together through thick and thin. Even Martine!' Mum got closer, so she was whispering in my ear. 'She won't go back, you'll see. She'll go off that dull boy Tony soon enough. She'll meet some nice new boy. It's plain as day in her charts.' Mum glanced out of the window uncertainly. 'Maybe not from round here. At her new school! She'll settle down and sit her exams and surprise herself by doing really well. I'm sure she's bright enough to go to college and make something of herself. I want all you girls to have proper careers. I don't want you just being a mum like me and doing rubbish jobs like cleaning and bar work. I reckon Martine could get a job in the City – one of these business women in Armani suits earning pots of money.'

'And Jude?'

We both had a giggle at the idea of Jude in a designer suit.

'Something outdoorsy and adventurous for our Jude. She could maybe be a skiing instructress or run her own stables.'

Jude had never strapped on skis or sat on a horse in her life, but we could both see her doing just that.

'And it's obvious Rochelle has to be an actress. She's got the looks and she's certainly enough of a drama queen,' said Mum.

'What about me, Mum? What am I going to do?'

'You're my little dreamer. Maybe you'll make up stories. Yeah, write books like those *Harry Potter*s. You can keep us all in the lap of luxury, eh?' Mum looked all the way round the room, and then shook her head. 'We'll get this place fixed up, Dixie. I know it's a dump but we've always got our home sorted and looking lovely, and we'll do it here too. It *could* be a lovely house, once it's all clean and painted. It's got nice big rooms so we'll have more space. And we've got the garden! You wanted a garden, didn't you, Dixie? Run out into the back garden, see what it's like. Quick, before Rochelle sees you.'

I ran through to the kitchen. Bruce was labouring at the sink, his face screwed up.

'Poor Uncle Bruce,' I said.

'Yeah, poor silly old fool Bruce,' he said, but he didn't stop scrubbing.

'Mum says I'm to check out the back garden,' I said. I scrabbled with the key in the back door.

'Hang on, I'll do it,' said Bruce.

'No, *I* can do it,' I said, wrenching the key and scraping

the skin off my fingers. I still couldn't get the door open though I pulled and pulled.

'There's a bolt at the top, little 'un,' said Bruce, peeling off one of his rubber gloves. He reached over me and tried to budge it. It was a struggle even for him.

'Doesn't look like the garden's used much,' he said, shoving the door hard. It opened. We saw outside. Bruce whistled. 'Understatement of the century,' he said.

It wasn't a garden at all. It was a jungle. The grass came right up to my waist. Brambles grew everywhere like crazy hedges, turning the whole garden into a maze. I gazed at purple and blue and yellow plants.

'Flowers!' I said.

'Weeds, darling,' said Bruce.

'*I* think they're flowers,' I said, wading through them.

'Careful! Steer clear of them nettles. You'll be in over your head if you don't watch out. Come back indoors, Dixie,' Bruce called.

'Not yet! It's lovely here,' I said, thrusting my way through shrubs and ferns. There were great white flowers that really were way above my head, shading me like umbrellas.

'You watch where you're stepping,' Bruce muttered, but he went back indoors.

I fumbled for Bluebell and helped her soar up into the air, flying round the umbrella flowers, sweeping round the brambles, skimming the long tangled grasses. I imagined a flock of parrots to keep her company. Monkeys climbed the trees, swinging from branch to branch. Lions stalked through the undergrowth but I snapped my fingers at them carelessly. They bowed their great heads and let me stroke their beautiful golden backs. The largest lion raised his nose, opened his mouth and roared right in my face, his hot breath scorching me. I didn't flinch, though Bluebell fluttered away as fast as she could.

I trekked on fearlessly through entire continents until I came up against the Great Wall of China. It was a real brick wall, marking the end of our garden. I tried several running leaps at it to hitch myself up on top. I scraped all up and down my arms and dropped Bluebell in the grass. I tucked her down my T-shirt, and leaped at the wall again, getting the knack of it now. I hung on tight, heaving one leg up, then the other.

I was up there, sitting on the Great Wall of China itself. I peered up and down the gravelled alleyway, looking for Chinese people and rickshaws and chop suey restaurants.

'This is your birthplace, Bluebell,' I whispered down my neck.

The alleyway looked disappointingly ordinary and English. There was black creosote fencing the other side, and if I craned my neck like a meerkat I could see over a big gate into another back garden. It was very very different from my jungle garden. The grass was bright green and mowed into stripes. They looked as if they'd been drawn with a ruler. The beds of flowers were impossibly neat too, planted in a pattern, each plant so perfect I wondered if they might be plastic.

Down at the end of the garden there was a swing. It looked very fancy, with a white canopy and a padded seat. I wondered how high you could swing on it. I *loved* swinging. Jude used to take me to the rec back at Bletchworth, but then all the junkies started hanging out there and so we had to stop going.

I looked longingly at the swing. I could jump down off the wall, run across the alley, nip through the gate and jump on the swing. I pretended I was perched on that padded seat, rocking backwards and forwards.

Then a little girl walked down the garden, straight to the swing. I blinked, wondering if I was making her up. No, she was real, a very clean, tidy little girl of about six. She had the neatest plaits tied with pink polka-dot hair ribbons, and a pink dress to match. I saw her knickers when she climbed on the swing. They were snowy white with pink lace round the legs. She had white socks too and white sandals. I saw the rubber soles as she started swinging. Even they were spotless. It was like she lived on another planet altogether where dirt had been banished.

I jumped down off my wall and ran across the alley. I went to the gate and stuck my chin over the top.

'Hiya!' I said.

She was so startled she nearly fell straight off the swing. She looked back towards her house anxiously. It didn't look real either. It was a big black and white house with a red pointy roof and flowers growing up a trellis in a regular pattern, like wallpaper.

'It's all right! I'm not going to hurt you. What's your name?'

She stopped swinging, her chin on her chest. 'Mary,' she said, in this tiny little voice.

'I'm Dixie,' I said. 'And this is Bluebell.'

She raised her head a little.

'Here she is,' I said, holding Bluebell out on one finger over the gate.

She sucked in her breath. 'A little bird!' she whispered.

'Yes, she's my budgie. Want to stroke her?'

Mary nodded. She slid off the swing and came over to the gate. I could see she'd been crying. Her blue eyes were very watery and her little lashes were spiky with tears. She sniffed, wiped her eyes carefully and then held up her hand. She had remarkably clean hands with pearly fingernails, as if she was fresh out of the bath. I wished my own fingernails weren't so grimy. I noticed my cardie cuffs were grey too. I turned them over to hide the worst of the dirt.

I dangled Bluebell over the fence. Mary could just about reach. She tickled the back of Bluebell's head with one delicate little finger. Then she stopped, looking worried.

'Is it . . . dead?'

'What? No!'

'It's cold like it's dead. My kitten's dead now.'

'Oh, how sad. Is that why you're crying?'

'No, it died weeks ago. It got run over. It was my fault. I was very bad.'

'Why was it your fault?'

'Mummy said I left the front door open.'

'But you didn't *mean* to.'

'No, I loved my kitten.'

'Did you have a funeral? I love funerals. I had this mouse once. It wasn't really a pet mouse, but I caught it and kept it in a box. I tried to make it a special little mouse house and I fed it lots of cheese but it kept trying to eat the cardboard box instead. I should have let it go free but I really wanted a pet and so I kept it and then it died. I turned the house into a coffin and painted it black with a tiny portrait of the mouse on the top in a little oval with REST IN PEACE underneath. I put the mouse in one of my socks and then lined the coffin with Mum's old silky petticoat and I had a proper funeral. My sister Jude came to it, though she said I was weird. She helped me dig a hole down the rec and we buried the mouse. I made a little cross out of lolly sticks. My other sisters teased me and said I was taking after my dad. He's an embalmer, you see. They always tease me. You know what sisters are like.'

She was staring at me as if I was talking a foreign language.

'Do you have a sister?'

She shook her head.

'I'll lend you one of mine if you like! I've got three.'

She took me seriously and shook her head, her little plaits bobbing on her shoulders. They were pulled so tight they looked like they might give her a headache. I could see a little blue vein throbbing on her forehead.

'Here,' I said, reaching right over the gate to untie a plait for her.

She stepped backwards, fending me off. 'No! Don't! You mustn't!'

'I'm only going to loosen your plaits and make them comfier for you.'

'No! Please don't. I'm not allowed to untie them,' she said.

'OK. Sorry. You've got very pretty hair. I wish mine was really blonde, not mouse. Rochelle's got blonde hair too. She's the sister next to me. I'm the youngest so far. Until my brother gets born. Have you got any brothers?'

'There's only me.'

'That must be so peaceful! And you get brand-new toys

and clothes and never have to take turns. You can have a go on your swing whenever you want.'

I waited hopefully, wishing she'd invite *me* to have a swing. She didn't take the hint.

I sighed, leaning further over the gate, though it was starting to cut into my chest. 'We're always arguing, us four. Soon we'll be five. Like I said, my mum's having a baby. She says he's going to be called Sundance but maybe she'll change her mind.'

'Is Sundance a real name?'

'Well, it's weird, isn't it? We've all got funny names. Not like Mary. That's a nice sensible name.'

'It's a holy name. Jesus' mother was called Mary. She was very very holy and good. But I'm not.' Mary hugged her chest. There were goose pimples on her little white stick arms.

'You're cold. Here, put my cardie on.'

I fiddled with the latch on the gate, and suddenly it swung open. 'There!' I said, marching in.

Mary looked very worried.

'It's OK. I'm not going to do anything. I won't even have a swing, not if you don't want me to. I just want to warm you up with my cardie.'

Mary hunched her elbows against her sides so I couldn't get her arms in the sleeves.

'Go on, I'm ever so warm.'

'I'm not allowed,' said Mary.

'Yes you are. I'm not *giving* you my cardie, it's just to warm you up a bit.'

Mary let her arms grow limp. I draped the cardigan round her.

'There! It's a lovely blue, isn't it? It's gone a bit bobbly now but it's still beautiful. My dad bought it for me. Do you have a dad, Mary?'

'Yes, but he drives a coach so he's not home much,' said Mary. 'I wish he was home all the time.'

'Never mind. I don't get to see my dad much at all. He doesn't live with us, see. But it's OK, not having a dad around, just so long as you've got your mum.'

Mary stayed very still. She shivered, even though she was smothered in my cardigan.

I looked over at the swing. I took a step towards it. Mary looked more and more worried.

'It's OK, Mary. I just want to play.'

'I'm not really allowed to have someone in to play,' she said. 'Mummy might be cross.'

'Ah. Is she in a bit of a mood, then?'

Mary nodded.

'Well, look, can I just have one teeny swing? Is that all right? You don't mind?'

Mary looked as if she minded very much but she didn't try to stop me. I sat on the white padded seat and kicked my legs. I soared upwards. It was just as good as I'd imagined.

'Wheeee!' I sang.

'Shh! She'll hear,' said Mary.

'OK, OK. Just one little swing more, then I'll go, I promise,' I whispered.

I held the ropes and thrust my feet forwards, flinging back my head until I felt wonderfully dizzy. I felt as if I was flying right over the garden and the red pointy roof. Bluebell flew with me, high into the sky.

Then I saw Mary hunched under my blue cardie. 'OK, it's all right, you can have a go now,' I said, jumping off.

I staggered. 'Hey, look at me, I'm drunk!' I reeled around, putting it on now.

Mary stared but then started giggling.

'You play at being drunk too, Mary. Pretend to fall over!'

She squatted down obediently but was careful not to crumple her clothes. 'Daddy got drunk once,' she said.

'My mum sometimes gets drunk. She gets ever so funny and giggly. But she doesn't drink now, because of the baby. I suppose I'd better go now. I'm helping her get the house sorted. She can't do much because she's so big. Thank you for letting me have a swing.'

'That's OK.'

'I'll have to take my cardie back now. Did it warm you up?'

'Yes.'

'There, I knew it would! Can I can come and play again?'

'Well. I suppose. If Mummy doesn't find out.'

'What's up with your mum then? Is she often in a bad mood?'

Mary blinked. Then she took a deep breath. 'No, she's a lovely mummy. She's the loveliest kindest nicest mummy in the whole world.'

'That's good,' I said. 'Well, bye, Mary.' I made Bluebell give Mary's nose a very gentle peck. 'That's the way budgies say goodbye,' I said.

Mary giggled. 'You are funny, Dixie.'

I pulled a silly face at her and staggered out of her garden, pretending to be drunk again. Then I dashed back across the alleyway, leaped up and over the wall at the very first go, and went back through the jungle.

'*My* mum's the loveliest, kindest and nicest,' I said to Bluebell. '*And* my dad.'

I pretended that Martine and Rochelle and even Jude didn't exist. I lived in a beautiful black and white house with a garden and a swing with my mum and my dad and my real budgie Bluebell. I had my very own bedroom with a sky-blue ceiling and a rainbow round each wall. The carpet was green as grass with an indoor swing so I could soar backwards and forwards across my room.

Mum and Dad loved each other for ever and they loved me too. They said they didn't want to risk having any more children, girls or boys, because they could never never never love them as much as me. Dad still worked in a funeral home, and maybe Mum worked there too, carefully dressing all the dead people and powdering their faces and combing their hair. Each night, if there were any lilies left over from Uncle Bruce's wreaths Mum would plait them into her long black hair and look like a flowery princess.

6

Mum didn't look like a princess when I went back indoors. She was scrubbing away at the toilet upstairs, sitting on the floor with her legs stuck out comically either side of the loo.

'Hey, babe,' she said. 'What have you been up to, eh?'

'I've been in the garden. And I've made friends with a little girl over the way.'

'That's nice, darling. OK, are you going to help your old mum?'

'Yep.' I rolled up my cardie sleeves and started trying to clean the basin. The taps were stiff with black grime that wouldn't come off.

'Try using an old toothbrush,' said Mum. 'There's some bathroom stuff in that cardboard box.'

I couldn't find any really old toothbrushes. Rochelle's pink toothbrush was a *bit* bristly.

'Rochelle will kill you,' said Mum, when I started scrubbing. 'So what's your new friend called?'

'Mary. She's very shy. But we played a bit. I think she likes me.'

'Is she about your age? You could go to school with her.'

'I don't want to go to school, Mum. I want to stay home and help you. I could look after the baby when he comes.'

'You need your education, pet.'

We heard Jude shouting outside. Boys were shouting too. There was a lot of swearing, mostly from Jude.

Mum sighed. 'It looks like living here is going to be an education in itself. Help me up, Dixie. I don't know what's up with Jude but she's effing and blinding fit to show us all up.'

I ran down the stairs in front of Mum. Martine had to catch hold of me as I ran for the door.

'Hang on, Dixie, there's a whole gang out there. It's not *safe*.'

'Jude's there,' I said, dodging past Martine.

There were six boys out in the street by the van. Four had hoodie jackets, the hoods pulled over their baseball caps so they looked like fierce birds with beaks. There was one big fat guy with a very rude phrase scribbled across his enormous sweatshirt. The last boy had dark curly hair and a black scarf and an earring, a bit like a pirate. He was standing with his hands on his hips, shaking his head at Jude, looking pitying. Jude was swearing away at him, not seeming to notice she was outnumbered. These weren't boys like the kids at Bletchworth. They were older, and much scarier.

Rochelle was standing beside Jude. She looked angry too, her cheeks bright pink, her eyes glittering. 'Will you just bog off!' she yelled. She wasn't yelling at the boys. She was yelling at Jude.

'Yeah, push off, big sister,' said Pirate Boy.

'OK, when you've stopped hitting on my little sister. Do you know how old she is? *Twelve!*'

'Shut up, Jude! I'm very nearly thirteen.'

'And very well developed too, darling,' said Big Fat Guy.

'You talk to her like that and I'll punch you straight in your fat chops,' said Jude.

He said worse. Some very rude things about Rochelle *and* Jude. Her fist clenched and she punched him right on the chin. He shook his head, looking dazed.

'Right, she's asked for it,' said one of the Hoodies. 'Let's teach the stroppy little cow a lesson.'

Two of his mates seized Jude by the shoulders and slammed her up against Bruce's van. Jude lifted her leg and tried to kick them, but the others caught her. The first Hoodie stepped forward, grinning.

'Leave her be, she's only a silly little kid,' said Pirate Boy.

Jude unwisely said something very rude and insulting back. Then she spat in the Hoodie's face. He clenched his fists. I screamed and started running, but someone pushed me out the way. This person elbowed his way through the boys. The biggest Hoodie lunged at him but he blocked the punch with an arm that seemed made of wood. Then he used this bionic arm to strike sideways at his ribs. The Hoodie fell to his knees, gasping.

'Now clear off!' he shouted. 'Leave these girls alone!'

They went running for it.

I stared at this amazing Superman. It was *Bruce*!

'Wow, Uncle Bruce, you were simply *brilliant*! That was just like a cartoon fight, *wham-bam-bash*! And it

67

was you doing all the bashing! You saved Jude from getting beaten up.'

'I didn't need saving,' said Jude sourly, sucking her fist. Her knuckles were bright red from punching the Big Fat Guy.

'Let's see that hand,' said Bruce.

'It's fine,' said Jude. 'Just keep your nose out of things, right?'

'*You* keep your bogging nose out of things, you stupid interfering pig!' Rochelle yelled. 'How *dare* you come charging up acting like a total idiot! You can't tell me who I can talk to!'

'He obviously wants to do a lot more than talk, idiot. He's way too old for you. And he looks a complete plonker too. What does he think he is, an extra in *Pirates of the Caribbean?*'

'I think he's really cool,' said Rochelle. 'And I think he liked me, until *you* mucked it up telling him how old I am.'

'Yeah, *twelve* – but you've got the brains of a six-year-old,' said Jude, poking Rochelle.

'Don't you dare start hitting me!' said Rochelle, pushing Jude.

'Someone needs to slap some sense into you! Can't you see what those boys are *like?*'

'You're just jealous because they were chatting to me, not you,' said Rochelle. 'You can't stick it if someone fancies me, Jude Diamond.'

'Oh for God's sake, stop being so *idiotic!*' said Jude, shoving her in exasperation.

Rochelle was wearing her best red suede high heels. She found it hard to balance on them at the best of times.

She tottered backwards and ended up on her bottom with her legs in the air.

Pirate Boy was still lurking at the end of Mercury Street. He was looking back over his shoulder. Rochelle went as red as her shoes. She swore furiously, staggered upright and flew at Jude, trying to scratch her face with her long fingernails.

'Hey, hey, cut it out, girls!' Bruce cried.

They both told him to mind his own bogging business and carried on fighting. Jude could normally floor Rochelle in seconds but now Rochelle was so angry she was almost a match for her. I screamed, begging them to stop. Martine pocketed her phone and tried to wade between them. Jude accidentally punched her on the shoulder. Martine whipped off her shoe and started trying to whack them both about the head.

'Stop it! Please stop it, you crazy girls!' Bruce shouted hoarsely.

'This will put a stop to it,' Mum gasped, waddling up to us with a brimming bucket.

Suddenly we were all drenched in soapy water, screaming, sobbing, soaking wet.

'My cardie's all wet! And Bluebell!' I wailed.

'How *dare* you, Mum!' Martine said furiously.

'If you're all going to act like little wildcats you'll get treated like them,' Mum retorted.

'*I* wasn't fighting, I was trying to stop them. Look, my mobile's soaked! I'll kill you if you've ruined it!'

'My best suede shoes! They're sodden! You've spoiled them. You've all utterly humiliated me. I hate you all!' Rochelle screamed.

'Shut up, you stupid little show-off, you're the one that

started all this,' said Jude. Her wet hair stuck flat to her head so she looked like a seal. She felt her face and looked at the smear of blood on her fingers. 'You've clawed me, you little cat!'

She gave Rochelle another push. Rochelle retaliated by trying to scratch her again.

'Mum, Mum, stop them!' I shrieked, shaking my wet hair out of my eyes.

Mum didn't seem to be listening to any of us. She let the empty bucket fall to the ground with a clank. She put her hands on her stomach. Her face screwed up.

'Oh no!' said Bruce. 'Are you all right?'

'No I'm not bloody all right,' Mum muttered. She made little whimpering noises, her eyes screwed up.

'Oh Gawd, it's not the baby, is it?' Bruce asked.

Mum nodded, bending right over. Water trickled down her legs, as if she'd wet herself.

Bruce took two steps backwards, greasy-white with shock. Martine stopped wiping her mobile and stared at Mum. Jude started biting her thumb, one cheek still bleeding. Rochelle stopped shrieking and stood still, patting her damp hair into place.

'It's not due yet, Mum,' said Martine.

'Can't help that,' Mum said, breathing out weirdly, blowing *whoo-whoo-whoo.*

'Stop it, Mum, you can't be actually having it!' said Rochelle. 'It must be indigestion or something.'

'Indigestion, my bottom,' Mum gasped, though she used another ruder word. 'My waters have broken. I'm having the baby now!'

'Oh God, oh God, what are we going to do?' Rochelle

said, staggering around on her silly suede heels. 'How can you have a baby *here*?'

'We'll need the bedding out of the van. And we've got the kettle. We need lots of hot water,' said Bruce.

'What for?' said Jude.

'I don't know. That's what they always do in movies – get clean linen and hot water,' said Bruce.

'I'm not in some stupid old cowboy film, you berk. I'm having my son in hospital. I'm not booked in anywhere yet but they can hardly turn me away when I'm about to give birth any minute,' said Mum. She straightened up, breathing more slowly. 'God! I'd forgotten what it's like. Right, I'd better dig out a nightie and my washing stuff. And make-up. And the little blue sleeping suit, the one with the tiny teddies, for his little lordship. And the big blue shawl. Go on, jump to it, girls, I haven't got much time, judging by the strength of these contractions.'

Bruce was shifting from one leg to the other, still horrified. 'You're going to hospital, you said?'

'Yes, of course I am. You'll drive me there, won't you? Because I'm not up to tottering off down the bus stop, matey.'

'Yes, of course I'll take you. But then I'll *have* to get cracking. You'll have to find someone else to look after the girls. I'm no use. They don't do a thing I say.'

'*I* do what you say, Uncle Bruce,' I said.

'One out of four isn't that promising, Dixie,' said Bruce, but he smiled at me. 'Anyway, let's get the rest of the furniture out the back of the van, girls, so your mum can stretch out properly. Or should we leave one of the beds so she can lie on that?'

'Not *my* bed! I don't want it getting all icky with blood and baby stuff,' said Rochelle.

My three sisters went to sort out the back of the van with Bruce. I let out my own breath like I was having a baby myself.

'It's OK, Mum,' I whispered. 'I think he might be staying. You can stop pretending now.'

'Mm?' said Mum, clutching her stomach again. 'Oh Gawd, here it comes already. Tell them to get a move on, Dixie. My boy's going to pop out here on the pavement at this rate.'

'You mean you're really having the baby now?' I said, my heart starting to thump.

'Oh lord, Dixie, don't be so daft. I'm not that great an actress,' said Mum, running her hands through her hair. I saw the beads of sweat on her forehead. She screwed up her eyes against the pain and started *whoo-whoo-whoo*ing again.

'Mum?' I said, getting really scared.

She clutched me tight, struggling to keep upright. 'Oh, Dixie. It hurts so. It's too quick. Everything's going wrong. It is going to be all right, isn't it? My boy's going to be all right?' She sounded just as scared as me.

I took a deep breath and put my arm round her. 'Don't you worry, Mum, everything's going to be fine,' I said. 'You know it is. It says so in the stars.'

7

'All right, all right, the van's ready,' said Bruce, wiping his forehead and looking at Mum anxiously.

'Any minute now!' said Mum.

Bruce gave a little moan.

'Don't worry, I'll keep my legs crossed,' said Mum.

'You'll have to have one of the girls with you just in case the baby starts coming when I'm driving,' said Bruce.

'I was *joking*,' said Mum.

'I'm not,' said Bruce.

'I'll come, Mum,' I said, holding her hand.

'Don't be so silly, sweetheart. They wouldn't let you in,' said Mum.

'I'll come,' said Jude, but she looked a bit queasy.

'You wouldn't even know which end it came out of,' said Mum, laughing, even though she was doubled up in pain. 'I know babies aren't your thing, Jude, don't worry.'

'They're not my thing either!' Rochelle said hastily.

'No, no, you three must stay at home.' Mum looked at Martine, pleadingly.

'*OK*,' said Martine, sighing. She took Mum's arm and helped her into the van.

'Now, darlings, you behave yourselves, right? You'll be OK, won't you? Jude, here's two tenners, you nip out to the nearest chippy for your tea. Then I want you to lock yourselves in until Martine gets back. No more chatting up the local lads, Rochelle. No fighting, Jude. No treks over the garden wall, Dixie chick. And no more quarrelling, do you hear me? Rochelle, I'm talking to you!'

'She hit me. Mum!'

'Yeah, and who did this? said Jude, tapping her cheek. But then she nodded. 'I promise we won't fight, Mum.'

Rochelle pulled a face, but muttered 'Promise' too.

'You promise you'll be all right, Mum?' I said, trying not to cry.

I couldn't stand seeing her with her face all crumpled up with pain. I'd never been in a hospital but I'd seen *Casualty* and *ER*. I imagined Mum on a trolley, her vast belly under one of those flimsy white gowns like a giant bib, while scary masked people cut her open.

'Will they cut you, Mum?' I asked.

'No, no, not if I can help it! I still want to wear a bikini when I get my figure back. Don't look so worried, Dixie, I'll be fine. I promise. I'll probably be back here this time tomorrow with your little brother all tucked up in my arms, OK?'

'So who's going to look after the girls while you're in hospital?' said Bruce.

Mum looked at him as if he was simple. 'You are, Bruce, babe.'

74

'Oh no. No, look, I made it clear right from the start. I've got to get back. I should have been back at the shop hours and hours ago. I can't hang around babysitting your girls.'

'We're not babies,' said Jude. 'You push off. We don't need you.'

'Yes, they do need you,' said Mum. She doubled up again. 'I haven't got time to argue. You take me to the hospital, Bruce. I haven't got a clue where it *is* but you'll have to get me there sharpish, mate.'

She started her *whoo-whoo-whoo*ing, so loudly she sounded like a steam train. Rochelle sniggered. I dug my elbow in her and she punched me hard.

'Cut it *out*,' Mum gasped, and then she lay back in the van. 'Oh God, I think it's coming.'

'Hang on,' Bruce said grimly, slamming the van door shut behind Martine and starting up the engine.

We could hear Mum moaning inside as the van hurtled away. Jude and Rochelle and I stood on the pavement, staring after her. An old lady in a headscarf and matted fleece and bedroom slippers came out of a house three doors away. She looked us up and down like we were monkeys at the zoo.

'Did they kick you out your old place then?' she said.

'No they didn't!' said Rochelle, flouncing.

'Don't kid me. I've never seen the like. Fighting and brawling in the street the minute you get here! You girls acting like alley cats and your mum practically giving birth in the gutter!'

'You mind your own business, you old bag,' said Jude.

'I'm complaining about you to the council. This used to be a decent estate. When me and my late husband moved in we were proud to live here. Now look at this dump. And it's used as a dumping bin too, for all you problem families.'

'We're not a problem family!' I said.

'Come indoors, Dixie, Rochelle,' said Jude, grabbing us and pulling.

When we'd shut the front door I looked at Jude. 'We're *not* a problem family, are we?' I said.

'Of course not.'

'That's what they called us at school,' I said.

'It was a crap school.'

'I liked it,' said Rochelle. 'I liked Bletchworth High too. It's not fair. I really liked it. Mr Mitchell was my best ever teacher and he said if I really put my mind to it I could pass all my exams and go to university, but with my looks maybe modelling school could be an option.'

'Yeah, yeah, Mr Mitchell was just a pervy old creep,' said Jude. 'You are so *thick*, Rochelle. You act like you know it all and yet you haven't a clue. Why do you think those boys were chatting you up, eh?'

'They *liked* me. And if you hadn't poked your nose in I'd have copped off with that dark guy with the earring,' said Rochelle, poking Jude.

'Don't you poke me with those poxy pointy nails! Look at my face! That old bag was right, you're just like an alley cat.'

'Don't you call me a cat, you cow!'

'Stop it!' I shouted. 'Please please please don't start fighting again.'

Jude and Rochelle stared at me. I don't usually go in for shouting.

'Who pulled your chain?' Rochelle said rudely, but she stopped poking Jude and let her arms dangle limply.

'Are you feeling left out, Dixie?' said Jude. 'You can join in the fight too.' She punched me very lightly in the chest.

I knew she was joking. I acted out staggering and sank down onto the dirty carpet, pretending she'd floored me. Jude waved her fists in the air in mock victory. Rochelle sniffed at us. Then I stood up and we all stood staring at each other, wondering what to do next.

'Mum'll be all right, won't she?' I said.

'Of course she will. She's used to having babies. She's had enough practice, after all,' said Jude.

'But she said it was coming too quickly.'

'That's good, isn't it?' said Rochelle. She started sniggering again. 'Imagine if it comes before she gets to hospital! How will old Bruce cope?'

'I hope she doesn't hook up with him, he's such a creep,' said Jude.

'I *like* him,' I said.

'He looks like a frog,' said Rochelle. She pulled a stupid froggy face that was *nothing* like my Uncle Bruce. 'He talks like a frog too, all croaky.'

'And he puffs up like a toad when he's trying to boss us about,' said Jude.

'No he *doesn't*! Look, he *protected* you from those horrible boys.'

'They *weren't* horrible,' Rochelle huffed.

'Don't start again,' I begged her. I looked up and down the dark hall. I tried the light switch. I clicked it up and I clicked it down. It didn't work.

'Oh no,' I said. 'The light bulb isn't working.'

77

Jude edged her way into the living room, where most of our furniture had been dumped in everyone's haste to empty the van. She switched on the living-room light switch. It wasn't working either.

'Uh-oh,' she said.

'There's no *light*,' said Rochelle. 'What are we going to do? We can't stay in the dark. Jude?'

'What do you expect me to do? Turn into a torch?' said Jude, biting the skin of her thumb.

'Maybe the light works upstairs?' I suggested.

'It's not working anywhere, stupid,' said Rochelle, but she still went clattering upstairs to check.

'We can't go to bed in the *dark*,' she said, running back downstairs.

'We haven't got the beds up there yet,' said Jude. 'Maybe we'd better all stay downstairs tonight. She put her arm round me, seeing I was shivering. 'It's OK, Dixie, it'll be like camping. Look, you two start hunting around for all the duvets and start sorting them out and I'll go out for some fish and chips. Put the kettle on, Rochelle.' She paused. She bit her thumb again.

Rochelle was having the same thought. She ran into the kitchen and tried fiddling with the switches on the filthy cooker. 'Oh God, nothing electric will work! We can't even have a cup of tea. Or a hot bath. Or watch the telly.'

'Maybe Uncle Bruce will fix the electrics when he comes back?' I said.

'Not if it's all switched off. Anyway, I don't think he's going to *come* back. I bet you he'll just dump Mum and Martine at the hospital and then do a runner,' said Rochelle.

'Well, good riddance. We'll find someone else to fix it. The council,' said Jude. 'If only Martine had left us her mobile I could ring them now. Tell you what, I'll find a phone box and give them a bell while I'm out for the fish and chips.'

'You don't know the number,' said Rochelle. 'Oh God, what are we going to *do*?'

'Stop panicking, Rochelle, you're frightening Dixie,' said Jude.

'Oh, poor little poppet,' Rochelle mocked. 'Why do we all treat her like a blooming baby? She's nearly as old as me. She just looks so stupidly immature.'

'And you *act* so stupidly immature,' I said.

'That's great, coming from a girl with a stuffed toy birdy friend perched on her finger,' said Rochelle, flicking at Bluebell.

'Cut it out,' said Jude. 'Now get cracking with the bed stuff, both of you.'

'I want to come with you, Jude,' I said.

'No, you're better off here. Especially if those lads Rochelle's so crazy on are lurking close by.'

'Yes, that's *why* I want to come too,' I said.

'Oh bless! You're going to protect me, Dixie?' said Jude. 'I'll be back soon. Don't look so worried.'

She waved at us jauntily, but her face was pinched and she took a very deep breath as she went out the door, like she was about to dive off a cliff.

Rochelle and I looked at each other when she'd gone.

'So now there are just the two of us,' I said. 'It's like one of those creepy detective stories where people keep disappearing.'

'Horror story, more like. How could Mum dump us

here? She's so *stupid*,' said Rochelle. She squeezed in and out the furniture, kicking it with her spoiled suede shoes. 'I can't stand her sometimes.'

'Shut up, Rochelle. She's in the middle of having a baby and it looks like it's going all *wrong*.'

'What is she doing having another baby when she's got all of us? Serves her right if she has a bad time. It might make her more careful,' said Rochelle, fumbling her way through cardboard boxes.

'*Don't!* Look, all sorts of stuff could be happening to her,' I said. I remembered all the childbirth scenes I'd seen on the television. I saw Mum panting, purple in the face, screaming out. I saw a hospital bed and blankets spattered with bright-red blood. I saw Mum lying very white and still, and then the sheets being pulled over her head.

'Don't *cry*,' said Rochelle. 'Look, help me, birdbrain! Shove that silly budgie up your jumper and get searching for the duvets. They must have got jumbled up with the clothes.'

'What if she dies?' I sniffed, mopping my eyes on someone's T-shirt.

'Stop it, that's *my* T-shirt. Don't wipe your snotty face with it. And stop that silly boohooing, she's not going to *die*. She's not ill, she's just having a baby.'

'Some women do die having babies.'

'Trust you to be so morbid. You obviously take after your stupid dad. Aha!' Rochelle found one of the duvets at the bottom of a box, under Mum's clothes. She pulled it out, but got distracted by Mum's silky black kimono. 'She went without her night things,' said Rochelle, stroking the soft black material. She bent her head and sniffed Mum's scent. 'I didn't mean that about hoping Mum has a bad time,' She whispered. 'I was just saying that because I was mad at her.'

'I know,' I said.

I wiped my eyes with my own cardie sleeve. Bluebell gave me a little nudge with her beak as I did so. I clambered over the beds. They were mostly in bits so they could fit easily in the van. 'Shall we just fix Mum's bed and then we could share it tonight, you, me and Jude?' I said.

'Yuck, I don't want to sleep with you two,' said Rochelle, but she helped me fiddle with Mum's bed all the same. We couldn't get the headboard to stay slotted in properly and the mattress was too heavy for us to lift onto the base without Jude.

'We could just use the mattress tonight,' I said.

'I don't want to be down on the floor. Something might crawl over me. This place is so filthy. There could be cockroaches. Or rats.'

I wished Rochelle hadn't said that. She seemed to be regretting it too.

'What will we do if there *are* rats?' she said, standing up on Mum's armchair.

'We could . . . hit them with your high heels?' I suggested.

'I'm not having my best shoes made all manky with bits of dead rat!' said Rochelle, stepping down again gingerly.

'OK, OK. Well. We'll have to get all your cats – you know, the white ones: Snowdrop and Sugar Lump and Ice Cream, and they'll see the rats and they'll go, "Ooh, yum yum, tasty rat nuggets for our tea," and gobble them all up.'

81

Rochelle giggled. 'You're so weird, Dixie. I never know if you're funny or just plain bonkers.'

'Definitely bonkers,' I said, and pulled mad faces, miming being a crazy person as we wrapped a sheet round Mum's mattress and smoothed out the duvet and puffed up all the pillows.

Rochelle needed to go to the loo and made me come up the stairs with her and wait outside the door. We'd been running all over the house earlier on but now it was much more scary by ourselves.

I used the loo myself. While I was sitting on it there was a sudden thump at the door.

'Dixie! Quick, come to the door with me,' Rochelle hissed.

'I can't, I'm still going! You answer it. It'll just be Jude, with our chips.'

'What if it isn't? What if it's those boys? Dixie, do you *really* think they'd hurt me? The really good-looking guy with the earring? Don't you think Jude was just jealous?'

'Jude isn't the least bit jealous of you, you know that,' I said, bouncing up off the loo.

There was another thump at the door.

'Dixie, *please*, come with me.'

'OK, OK.' I rushed out of the loo, pulling my knickers up. 'Listen, we won't *open* the door, we'll shout first to see who it is. Only don't get too near the letter box or they could reach through and grab you.'

'Oh help help help, I *hate* this. Why can't we have an ordinary mum who looks after us and a proper dad and a *nice* house?' said Rochelle.

'I'd sooner be us Diamonds,' I said.

Rochelle and I edged towards the front door. We found we were holding hands.

There was another *thump-thump-thump*, loud and angry.

'Oh God,' said Rochelle. 'It *is* those boys. They've come to get me.'

'You boys can just bog off or my Uncle Bruce is going to get you,' I yelled.

The letter box opened. 'It's me, Jude! Why won't you open the door?'

We struggled to open it, our hands slippery with sweat.

'You two bananas,' said Jude, scoffing at us.

'It's not *our* fault. Why did you knock like that? Why couldn't you just let yourself in like a normal person? You just wanted to frighten us,' Rochelle sniffed.

'I couldn't let myself in, idiot, I don't have a key. Mum's got them all,' said Jude.

We stood still, thinking. We didn't even know where she *was*. Perhaps this town didn't even have a hospital. Maybe Bruce was driving round and round with Mum screaming in the back of his van . . .

'What if she doesn't come back tomorrow?' I said.

'Shut up, both of you,' said Jude. 'Let's eat. I got Coke too. And look, matches!' She held them up proudly.

'Have you got cigarettes then?' said Rochelle.

'No, you dumbo, it's so we can see when it gets dark.'

'Quit calling me names. You're the dumbo, you'll set the whole house on fire if you start playing around with matches. Why didn't you get a torch?'

'They don't sell bogging torches down the chip shop or the off-licence. I'm sure we've got candles somewhere in the kitchen box.'

We looked for them, without any luck.

'Maybe we can go and ask a neighbour for some?' Jude suggested.

'Oh yeah, like that old lady,' said Rochelle.

'Anyway, let's eat, for God's sake. The fish and chips are getting stone cold,' said Jude.

We ate them straight out of the paper because we didn't know where the plates were. We took turns swigging Coke out of the bottle. We used the rolled-up carpet as a table and chair.

'These chips aren't anywhere near as nice as the ones from our chippy at home,' Rochelle complained.

'Well, I'm sorry, Lady Muck. I should have trudged sixty miles all the way home to get chips more to your taste,' said Jude. 'Give us yours, then, I'm still starving.'

Jude finished up eating most of mine too. 'Doesn't Bluebell want any chips?' she asked.

'Oh, don't start her off. She doesn't half get on my nerves with that stupid toy bird,' said Rochelle.

'You get on *my* nerves,' I said. 'You just whinge and whine and moan moan moan but you don't help get things organized.'

'Oh yeah? So what's *your* major contribution, Ms Brain-dead Queen?' said Rochelle.

'I know a neighbour we can ask for candles,' I said proudly.

Jude and Rochelle stared at me.

'No you don't, stupid,' said Rochelle.

'I *do*. My friend Mary lives at the back of our garden. We can ask her mum. She says she's ever so kind,' I said.

Rochelle snorted. 'Oh God, she's really gone crackers

now. There are little friendies at the bottom of our garden! You'll end up in a loony bin if you don't watch out, Dixie.'

'She's real. I played with her in the garden. *I did!*'

Rochelle raised her eyebrows and sighed. 'My sister, the nutcase,' she said.

'You come and see,' I said, crumpling up my chip paper and throwing it at her.

'Yuck! Stop it, you'll get my top all greasy;' said Rochelle. 'I'm not going out into that jungle out the back. There'll be all sorts hiding in the grass – mice, toads, snakes.'

'I'll come with you, Dixie,' said Jude.

'No, don't! Don't leave me by myself!' said Rochelle.

'*Now* who's the baby?' said Jude. 'You'll have to stay, Rochelle, as we haven't got a door key. Besides, Martine will be coming back sometime.'

'I bet she doesn't. I bet she hitches a lift back to Bletchworth. She's not daft. I wish I could go with her.'

I wished she would too. I thought how peaceful it would be, just Jude and me. And Mum, of course. Though now there would be the baby too.

'It's all the baby's fault,' I said, as Jude and I went out the front door. 'If Mum hadn't got pregnant she wouldn't have wanted the extra room and we wouldn't have moved. I hope little Sundance is extra sweet or I shall seriously dislike him.'

'Sundance! I hope Mum's joking,' said Jude. 'No, it's not *his* fault. He didn't ask to be born, did he? I don't know why Mum wants to keep on having all these boyfriends and babies. I just don't get her.'

'Yeah, I know. But Mum says she's finished with

blokes now,' I said, skipping along beside Jude.

'As if!' said Jude.

'Well, if you get your Rottweiler – you know, to chase away Rochelle's white cats – then he'll maybe chase all the boyfriends away too.'

'That was just a game, Dix.' Jude turned round and looked at me. 'So this Mary, is she a game too?'

'No, she's real, I *said*. Look, see over the wall? That's her house. Doesn't it look clean and tidy? Mary's so clean and tidy too.'

I checked the grey cuffs on my cardie, the stain on my T-shirt, the hems of my jeans, black and fraying where they trailed on the ground. 'Jude, are we dirty?'

'What? Well, you're a bit grubby, certainly. *I'm* clean. Cleanish. And Rochelle's never out the blooming bathroom. Ditto Martine.' Jude climbed onto the wall. She stood right up on it, legs braced. 'So that's your Mary's house then? Wow!'

'The one opposite, with the black wooden fence. Jude, be *careful.*'

She'd started to tightrope-walk along the top of the wall, showing off.

'Whoops, whoops, I'm falling to my death,' Jude said, waving her arms around, winding me up.

'Stop it!'

What if something really happened to Jude? I imagined her pitching off the wall and breaking her neck. All my family was disappearing. I only had Rochelle left, and I didn't even like her . . .

'Dixie?' Jude held out her hand. 'Come on, don't look so worried. I'm only messing about, you know I am.'

'What about Mum?' I said.

'Mum will be *fine*,' said Jude, though she didn't sound sure. 'Come on, don't let's think about Mum just now. She'll be back safe and sound with the baby soon, you wait and see. Tomorrow. So let's get ourselves sorted out now, right? We'll go and see if your pal Mary's mum will give us some candles.'

Jude helped me over the wall into the alleyway. I stopped her as we got to Mary's back gate.

'Maybe we ought to go to the front?' I said. 'We can't just barge right into their back garden, can we?'

'Why not?' said Jude. She stood at the gate, looking across the neat green lawn. There were no toys scattered, no balls or bikes, no one sitting on the beautiful canopied garden swing.

'If we just wander in then Mary's mum might think we're burglars,' I said.

'OK, OK, we'll go round to the front and knock, if it makes you happy,' said Jude.

I don't think she was too keen on marching over that weirdly perfect lawn either.

We went down the alleyway to the end, turned left, and then went back down Mary's street. It was as if we'd walked into a different world altogether. The houses were *all* tidy and clean and freshly painted, with shiny door knockers and little porches and ruffled curtains at the spotless windows.

'I wish *our* house looked like these,' I said. 'Do you think they're one of the other planets?'

'No, silly, these aren't council houses, these are private. They're posh, can't you tell? Is Mary posh?'

I considered. I started to worry. 'She's not *snooty* posh,' I said.

'Which is her house, then?' Jude asked.

I couldn't work it out. I peered at the rows of identical black and white houses. I didn't know how to match up the fronts with the backs.

'It's this one,' I said, pointing at the nearest.

Jude clicked open the metal gate. I tugged at her sweatshirt.

'No! Next door. Or the one after. I don't *know*,' I said.

Jude sighed. 'What are you like, Dixie?' she said. 'Come on, which is it?'

I dithered. 'Maybe we should go back and try the back way after all?'

'Maybe we'll just knock on any old front door and *ask*,' said Jude.

She went in the next gate along. The hedge was growing out across the pavement and the car on the front drive was red and sporty.

'Not that one, Jude. This might be it,' I said, nodding at the next house with the metal gates. The hedge was clipped into a green wall, not a leaf out of place. It reminded me of Mary's plaits.

Jude swung the gate open and started walking up the crazy paving path. I hung back.

'What are you waiting for? She's *your* friend,' said Jude.

I trailed after her, wishing I'd held my tongue about Mary.

'Come *on*,' said Jude irritably.

She rapped loudly with the lion door knocker. We waited. My heart was beating as if I had a little knocker right inside my chest. Then the door opened, although the lady looking at us kept one hand on the latch so that she could slam it shut in a second.

She was very pretty, with lovely golden hair curling almost to her shoulders and very blue eyes. They were outlined with grey pencil, very carefully, without a single smudge. Her skin was peachy with powder, her lips pearly pink. Mum didn't often bother to do her face if she was staying in during the day, but she wore lots of black eye make-up and deep red lipstick when she went out on the razzle.

Mary's mum didn't look as if she'd do any razzling down the pub or the club. She was wearing a pink fluffy sweater and a white pleated skirt. She looked like a mum in a telly advert, the sort who'd make a meal on her cooker and then serve it up on a tablecloth.

She looked at Jude, she looked at me. 'Yes?' she said.

I swallowed hard. I tried to say something but only a mouse squeak came out.

'My sister's friends with your daughter,' said Jude.

'I don't think so,' she said.

'I'm her new friend,' I whispered.

She was shaking her head. Jude glared at me, thinking I'd made it all up after all.

'You're Mary's friend?' she said.

I took a deep breath, nodding.

'Where did you meet her? At school?'

I hesitated.

'They were playing together in your garden,' said Jude, not realizing she might be getting Mary into trouble. 'We've just moved in. We're on the Planet Estate.'

Mary's mother nodded, watching me with her corn-flower-blue eyes. She looked like a princess in my fairy story book.

'So Mary invited you into our garden?' said her mum.

I knew I had to be very careful. 'Well, no, I was in that lane at the back of our house and your house. Mary was in *your* garden. I talked to her.'

'Ah,' said Mary's mum. 'Well. That's very nice. I'm glad you've made friends. But I'm afraid she can't come out to play just now, dear. She's not very well so I've sent her to bed early.'

'Well, we really came round to ask you a favour,' said Jude.

'Oh?' said Mary's mother warily.

'I – I wonder if you could loan us—' Jude started.

'No, I'm sorry, dear,' she interrupted. 'I'm afraid I never give to anyone at the door.'

'We're not *begging*,' said Jude, fiery red. 'We don't ever beg. We were just wondering if you'd loan us a candle because the lights aren't working in our house.'

'A candle?' said Mary's mum. She looked surprised. Then she smiled. 'Yes, of course. Wait here a minute.' She shut the door on us.

'Why won't she let us in after her? Does she think we're going to nick her ornaments? Blow this. Blow *her*. Come on, Dixie, let's go back,' said Jude.

We started down the pathway again.

The door opened. 'Hey, girls! I thought you wanted a candle,' said Mary's mum. She was holding a whole packet of them, with some matches too.

'Thank you very much,' I said, bobbing back. 'We've already got matches, but thank you for the thought.'

She smiled as I took the candles, looking prettier than ever.

'Maybe Mary can come and play tomorrow?' I said.

'Maybe,' she said, still smiling.

She closed the door again. I waited, counting the candles.

I heard her in the hall, calling for Mary. Then I heard a sharp slap and someone crying.

8

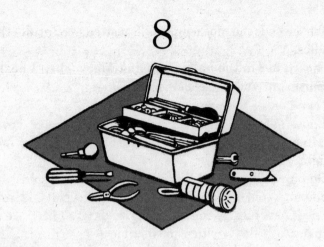

'You mean pigs! You've been gone such ages!' said Rochelle. 'I thought you weren't ever coming back. And it's getting dark and what are we going to *do*?'

'Candles!' I said, jiggling them at her. 'From my friend Mary's mum.'

I shivered. I hadn't told Jude about the slap or the crying. It seemed too private and shameful. I didn't see how anyone could hit a little girl like Mary. Maybe I'd made a mistake. I didn't *see* the slap, I only thought I heard it. Perhaps Mary tripped over, bumped herself and started crying. Her mum couldn't have hit her. She was the kindest sweetest mother in all the world.

I wondered about my own mum. 'Do you think Mum's had the baby yet?' I asked. 'How long does it take?'

'Don't ask me,' said Jude, with a shudder.

'It can take ages. Days, sometimes,' said Rochelle. 'It's the worst pain you can ever imagine. Far far far worse than the worst period pain ever, though of course *you* wouldn't know about that, Dixie.'

I thought about my worst pain ever, when some girls at my old school had punched me in the stomach until I was sick. I wondered what it would feel like to be punched in the stomach for days on end.

I cuddled in to Jude.

'*Baby*,' said Rochelle, but when we all flopped down on Mum's bed she wanted to cuddle up too. 'It's *Pop Idol* tonight,' she whined.

'Go on, we'll pretend like it's on the telly,' I said.

'You and your pretending, Dixie,' said Rochelle, raising her eyes to the dingy ceiling. 'Yuck! Look, it's filthy! We're all going to go down with some terrible disease like rabies.'

'You get rabies from mad dogs, you nutter,' said Jude. She bared her teeth and started growling and slavering at her.

'It's *scabies*. A boy in my class back at Bletchworth had them. Then I fell over and hit my head and had scabs and the teacher thought *I'd* got them,' I said.

I wondered what the school would be like here. Probably the kids would be even nastier, the teachers even meaner.

'*Sing*, Rochelle,' I said.

She started working her way through old Britney and Beyonce numbers, standing on the bed and wiggling her bottom. Jude and I cheered her at the end of each song and gave her glowing reviews. Jude's were way over the top, saying stuff like Rochelle had the voice of an angel and the figure of a she-devil, sending her up. Rochelle took her ultra-seriously and started preening, prancing all round the room.

Then she started singing one of Mum's old favourites, that weird Queen song like an opera with lots of strange

93

words like Beelzebub and Galileo. We tensed up when she got to the 'Mama Mia' part. Rochelle stopped at the second Mama and rubbed her lips, as if she could wipe the sound away.

'This is stupid,' she said, flopping down on the bed.

It suddenly seemed very very quiet in the house. It was starting to get dark. I thought of all the tough boys on the estate, out on the prowl. I thought of the men who'd broken into this house and drunk themselves crazy and puked in the sink.

'Shall we push the cupboard against the door so no one can get in?' I whispered.

'What about the window?' said Rochelle. 'They could simply smash it and climb in.'

'No one's going to break in – but if they do I'll fight them off,' said Jude. 'Let's play the television game again. I know, I'll be *Match of the Day*.'

She jumped up and started dodging in and out of the crowded furniture, kicking a rolled-up sweater and yelling, '*Here's Jude Diamond with the ball, running with it – look at the girl go . . . talent on wheels, dodging, feinting . . . Come on, Diamond – yes, you can do it! She's diving at the net – yes, smack in the middle! What a goal – the girl done good, the Diamond sparkles!*' Jude jumped up and down between the boxes, waving her hands in the air.

'Right, Dixie, your turn,' she said.

'Don't do something wet wet wet on little kids' telly,' said Rochelle.

'I'm going to do a nature programme. And it *is* wet wet wet because it's a tropical jungle,' I said, getting off the bed and crouching low.

I clutched a hairbrush like a mike and started whispering into it, like that old man David Attenborough.

'*So here we are, in this hot steaming jungle, on the track of the lost tribe of giant gorillas,*' I whispered. I took Bluebell out of my sleeve and made her flutter past my face. '*Birds of Paradise flash their rainbow wings,*' I said. I took Jude's sweater-football and perched it on my shoulder, one sleeve swinging. '*Mischievous monkeys leap all around me, wanting to make friends.*' I made the sweater chatter and scratch. '*But remember, we are on a quest for the lost tribe of giant gorillas – and* hist! *I hear growling!*'

'Gorillas don't growl,' Rochelle muttered. 'They're shy and gentle.'

'Pipe down, we're watching Dixie,' said Jude.

I carried on winding my way in and out the furniture, my hand cupped behind my ear. 'Definite *growling,*' I whispered. '*Which is distinctly odd, because world gorilla expert Rochelle Diamond has led us to believe that gorillas do* not *growl. She has appeared on my programme, giving us the benefit of her knowledge, informing us all again and again and again that gorillas are sweet, shy creatures that wouldn't say boo to a goose – but* I *think the growling sounds very aggressive. It's coming from over here. Could this be a giant gorilla lair?*'

'They don't live in *lairs*, idiot. They build nests in trees,' said Rochelle.

'In *trees?*' said Jude. 'Jeez, I wouldn't want to be walking underneath in case they turned over too quickly and fell out of their nests. Imagine being squashed to death by a furry gorilla.'

I was scrabbling in Mum's clothes bag for her fun-fur

winter coat. I shoved it over my head, then jumped up on top of two boxes and thumped my chest. 'Grr! Grr! I am the leader of the lost tribe of giant gorillas! I don't give a toss what Rochelle says about *other* gorillas. I am very very very aggressive and I hate know-all girls who think they're clever and I'm going to *get* her!' I leaped right on top of Rochelle on Mum's mattress, growling fit to bust.

Rochelle squealed and tried to fight me off, the fur coat slipping so that neither of us could see. There was a loud banging somewhere. We both struggled up out of the coat depths, wondering what Jude was up to. But Jude was sitting up too, listening.

'Jude?'

'Someone's knocking at the door,' she said.

They banged again, fiercely, insistently. Two people knocking, one using their fists. Then someone opened the letter box and shouted through it.

'Open the door, you dozy lot!'

Martine! We ran to the door, Rochelle and I stumbling over Mum's fur coat. Jude got there first and slung the door open. Martine and Bruce stood there.

'At last!' said Martine.

'You've come back, Uncle Bruce! I knew you would. But where's Mum?'

'She hasn't had the baby yet,' said Martine wearily. She'd smudged her eye make-up so that she had great panda eyes, and her hair was sticking up in clumps.

'But it was practically popping out in the van!' said Jude.

'Apparently it slowed down once she was in the hospital. The nurse I spoke to said she wasn't in strong

96

labour yet so we might as well go home,' said Bruce, rubbing his eyes and yawning. 'Look, I've *got* to get to *my* home now, girls.'

'Not strong labour!' said Martine, her fists clenched. 'It was so strong she was screaming. She was in agony!'

'Now, now, no need to go upsetting your sisters,' said Bruce. 'I'm sure she'll be fine. She had all of you OK, didn't she?'

'No she didn't. She nearly died having Dixie,' said Martine, glaring at me like it was my fault.

'Well, the nurse said she was doing fine – everything under control and proceeding normally. She wouldn't have fibbed to me, especially as she thought I was the father.' Bruce shook his head, sighing.

'I don't know why she even spoke to you. You're nothing to do with our family,' Martine said furiously.

'Yeah, well, I'm starting to go down on my knees and count my blessings on that one,' said Bruce. 'I don't know why you're all turning on me. I've gone out of my way to be helpful, and given up a whole day's work for you – for no financial recompense whatsoever, it seems. I've acted like a blooming saint, and yet you've all taken advantage of me.'

'I haven't, Uncle Bruce,' I said, taking his hand. 'Do you want some of my chips? I couldn't eat them all. They're a bit cold now but maybe you don't mind?'

'Thank you, sweetheart. No, I think I'll give your chips a miss. One of you big girls could go and make me a nice cup of tea though. I think we could all do with a cuppa while we try and sort out who's going to look after you.'

'*I'll* look after us. And you can't have a cup of tea, so there,' said Jude.

'She's not being rude,' I said quickly (though she was). 'It's just the electrics don't work in the house and so we can't plug the kettle in. We've got candles though. I got them, from my friend's house. Maybe if we lit them all and held them under the kettle it would start boiling.'

'It's your head that needs boiling, Dixie, you're so stupid,' said Rochelle.

'The electrics?' said Bruce, sighing. 'Let's see. Where's the fuse box?'

'Don't look at me. It's not *my* house,' said Martine. 'As soon as Mum's back and better, I'm off. This is a total *dump*. We got a bit lost and couldn't find Mercury at first, so we've been all over the bogging Planets, and they're all awful. There were some little boys peeing in the street, and some big lads – real thug types – whizzing all over on skateboards.'

'One damn near went smack into my van. Could have killed himself, but he just laughed!' said Bruce.

'*Some* parts are lovely,' I told him. 'Right at the back of our house there's this lane and some *beautiful* houses. What sort of house do you live in, Uncle Bruce?'

He wasn't listening. He was opening up a little cupboard in the hallway and peering into it. He sucked his teeth and then walked down the hall and opened the front door.

'Don't go yet!' I called.

'I'm just getting my tool box from the van, Dixie,' he said. 'But then I'll *have* to go, sweetheart. You'd better all be thinking who you're going to call. Have you got a nan?'

'She died. She didn't like us much anyway,' said Jude.

'She never even sent us birthday or Christmas presents

– imagine!' said Rochelle, tossing her hair and striking a tragic attitude.

'My heart bleeds for you,' said Bruce.

I *loved* the way he didn't seem to think much of Rochelle. I followed him out to his van. He found his tool box and lugged it out of the van.

'Do you think you can fix the electrics, Uncle Bruce?'

'I'll have a go,' he said. He took his big glasses off and gave the lenses a wipe on the bottom of his T-shirt. His face looked younger without them, though they left pink pinch marks on his nose.

'I used to wear glasses,' I said. 'Mum thought I couldn't see the board properly at school.'

'So did your eyesight get better?'

'No, some kid tripped me in the playground and my glasses broke and we didn't ever get them mended,' I said.

Bruce was frowning. 'Does your dad pay maintenance for you, Dixie?'

I shrugged. 'I don't know.'

'Maybe your mum could get the social services to pay for new glasses for you?'

'Oh no, I don't want them. They called me Goggle-Eyes at school.'

He put his own glasses back on, wincing. 'Snap! That's what they called me when *I* was at school,' he said.

'I hate school,' I said.

'Maybe this new school will be better?' he said, going back into the house.

'Maybe,' I echoed, though it didn't seem likely.

I *could* look out for my new friend Mary in the playground though.

I thought about that slap behind the closed door. I felt sad and wanted Mum.

Then I thought *properly* about Mum.

What was happening to her now?

'Don't look so sad, sweetheart,' said Bruce. He chucked me awkwardly under the chin. 'I bet school will be a doddle.'

'I'm not thinking about school now,' I said. 'I'm thinking about Mum.'

'Well, tell you what,' said Bruce, as I trotted after him. 'How about if I phone your dad? Maybe he could come and look after you for a few days?'

I so wanted to believe this could be true. 'I don't think so,' I said mournfully. 'He's got his other family.'

'Yes, well, you're family too.'

'But they don't know about Mum or me, see,' I mumbled.

'Ah. Well. Yes, I suppose that does make a difference,' said Bruce. 'It doesn't really let him off the hook though. He's still responsible. But under the circumstances we'd better not pester him. So, what about the other girls' dads?'

He started peering at the fuse box, taking stuff out and getting things out of his tool box. Jude came to watch, irritated that he seemed to know what to do.

'You'd be mental if you got in touch with *my* dad,' said Jude, peering. 'If you even knew where to track him down. Where do they put violent nutters? Broadmoor, maybe?'

'Oh well, it's good you don't take after him,' said Bruce. 'Pass us that screwdriver, Judy.'

'*Jude!*' said Jude crossly, but she did as he asked. She

held his torch for him so he could see into the gloomy box. He told her what he was doing and why. It was all gobbledegook to me, but Jude nodded, taking it in. Then Bruce flicked a switch inside the box, told me to try the hall light – and it worked!

'Well done, Uncle Bruce! You're brilliant!' I yelled.

'No, I'm not. Any fool could fix it,' said Bruce. 'You can do it if it ever happens again, Jude.'

'You calling me a fool?' she said, but she was only joking.

Martine came running from the bathroom, where she'd been washing her face. 'You've really fixed it!' she said. 'Does that mean the water will be hot now?'

'Well, we'll give it a go. Let's hope the boiler isn't bust. I doubt if I can fix that,' said Bruce. He stepped nearer Martine. 'Jude here says it's no use contacting your dad because he's a bit violent?'

'*My* dad isn't a bit violent – but the last we heard he's in Australia,' said Martine.

'We've all got different dads,' I said.

'Oh Gawd, your family isn't half complicated,' said Bruce, shutting up the fuse box. He nodded at Rochelle, who was rushing round the house switching on every single light.

'Don't go too mad, you'll overload the system again,' he called. 'So, Dixie, what about Princess All-too-pleased-with-herself? What's *her* dad like?'

'Dead,' I said. I paused. 'That's how my mum met my dad.'

Bruce raised his eyebrows. 'She's a one, your mum!'

I looked at him sideways. Rochelle switched the light on and off, on and off. Jude stood up straight, her chin in the air. Martine ran her fingers through her wild hair, glaring at him.

'Are you having a go at our mum?' she said, speaking for all of us.

'No! No, I was – admiring her, like. For – for getting on with life. I wish I could say the same.' Bruce blinked anxiously behind his big glasses.

I nodded at him. 'Tell us about your life, Uncle Bruce.'

'Nothing much to tell,' he said.

'Have you got children?'

'No, no.'

'Have you got a partner?'

'Not at the moment, no. No family to speak of.'

I gave him a great big smile. 'You could be part of *our* family, Uncle Bruce,' I said very quickly, before the others could stop me.

'Well, that's very very sweet of you, Dixie. I'm touched. But no – I mean, you've got your lives to lead, I've got mine. Such as it is. Anyway, I *must* get back. I'll just check the immersion. Gawd, they don't half install some rubbish in these council gaffs.'

'I suppose you live in a bogging palace,' said Martine.

'Well, it's hardly that, but it's a good solid semi – Victorian. It was my mum and dad's house, see. I grew up there. I've tried to keep everything in good nick. It's got a fair-sized garden, little rockery, vegetable patch at the end—'

'Yeah, yeah,' Martine interrupted.

'He sounds like an estate agent,' Jude whispered, too loudly.

Rochelle sniggered and tapped the immersion. 'Have you got it working? Because I want a bath,' she said.

'I'm not the general servant, you know,' said Bruce, running the kitchen tap. 'You girls should keep civil tongues in your heads if you want folk to help you. There!' He put his hand under the tap and lightly sprayed Rochelle. 'Warm enough for you?'

Bruce straightened up, unrolling the cuffs of his check workshirt. He let the sleeves hang down over his pink hands. 'Well, I'm off, girls. I reckon you'll have to cope by yourselves until your mum comes back from the hospital.'

'We can't cope, Uncle Bruce. Don't go!' I said, rushing to him.

I jumped up and put my arms round his neck. He took one little step backwards, looking startled, but then his arms came round me and he gave me a little hug. He smelled of sandlewood talcum powder and toffees, such a gentle, reassuring smell that I couldn't help clinging when he tried to unhook my hands.

'God, stop acting like a *baby*,' said Rochelle.

'Why are you making such a fuss? You hardly know him,' said Martine.

'Cut it out, Dixie!' Even Jude was irritated with me.

I couldn't help it. I felt like a baby. I couldn't stop fussing. I couldn't cut it out.

'You'll be OK, little 'un. Oh, there now, don't cry!' Bruce reached in his trouser pocket and brought out a very old-fashioned clean white handkerchief, carefully ironed into a square. 'Here, dear, blow on this.' He tried to blow my nose for me, without much success.

'I'll make it all mucky,' I said.

'Never mind, that's what it's for. You keep it,' he said. He looked at Martine. 'Look, I really *have* to go.'

'I know. Go on, then,' she said.

'I didn't mean to get into all this. I was just doing a favour for a pal.'

'My dad,' I sniffled.

'He's a lucky guy having a lovely little kid like you for his daughter,' said Bruce. He bit his lip, struggling with something. 'Tell you what. I'll go home now. I've got to see about the shop and do stuff, but I'll come back tomorrow. I could come back to your place late morning, say. Then I'll take you all over to the hospital and your mum will have had the baby by then and you can all meet your little brother. OK?'

'You bet it's OK, Uncle Bruce!' I said.

The other three nodded too. Jude even muttered 'Thank you.' Bruce nodded back, waved his hand awkwardly in the air, and then practically ran out of the house.

'Isn't he lovely?' I said.

'No!' said Martine.

'He's OK, I suppose,' said Jude.

'He's OK if you don't mind him looking and acting like a total geek,' said Rochelle. She twitched her nose and stuck her front teeth over her bottom lip, doing a cruel Bruce imitation. Martine and Jude giggled.

'Well, *I* think he's lovely,' I said. 'He's my third favourite grown-up, after Mum and my dad.'

Martine found the kitchen cardboard box and made a pot of tea. We ate a packet of biscuits between us. I felt sad we hadn't got around to making Bruce anything, especially as he had that long drive back. I decided I'd keep the kettle boiling all Sunday morning so that he could have a cup of tea the moment he got here.

Martine tried phoning the hospital on her mobile but

it took ages for her to be put through to the right ward and then they said they could only give information to Mr Diamond.

'Well, there isn't one,' said Martine furiously, and zapped the phone off.

'Mum is all right though, isn't she?' I said. 'I mean, they'd have said if – if—'

'Of *course* Mum's all right,' said Martine. 'Stop being such a worryguts. Everything's fine.'

She was scared too though. I heard her get up very early in the morning and rush to the toilet. She shut the door, but I heard her being sick. She was shivering when she got back into bed.

'Are you all right, Martine?' I whispered.

'Ssh! You'll wake the others,' Martine hissed.

I couldn't get back to sleep. I don't think Martine did either. She tried to cuddle Rochelle to get warm, but Rochelle kept tossing and turning, digging into me with her bony elbows, suffocating me with her long curly hair. I cuddled up as close as I could to Jude, Bluebell clutched tight against my chest.

I don't think I've ever wanted Mum so much in all my life.

9

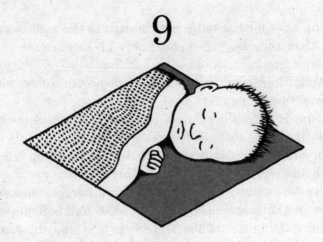

I heard a car draw up outside at ten o'clock the next morning.

'It's Uncle Bruce! He's here already!' I cried joyfully, running to the door. I opened it and stared.

It wasn't Bruce at all.

It was Mum getting out of a taxi. Our mum, back already, holding a blue blanket bundle in her arms.

I went flying out to her. 'Mum! Mum! Oh, Mum, you're all right!'

'Hey! Careful, Dixie! Watch out, you'll have me over. Mind the baby!'

Mum was holding the blanket close to her chest. I could just see a little tuft of black hair.

'Let's see him, Mum!'

Mum's face tightened, as if she was still in pain.

'Mum? What is it?'

'I'm sore, sweetheart, seeing as I've just had a baby,' she said.

'That'll be nine pounds eighty pence please,' said the cab driver.

'Gawd, for that piddly drive? I'd have been better off waiting for an ambulance,' said Mum. 'Here, Dixie, fish in my bag for my purse and give the guy a tenner. You can keep the change.'

'Oh, very generous, I'm sure,' said the cabbie.

I found the money and gave it to him.

'Thanks, darling,' said Mum, still hugging the baby close.

I was starting to worry terribly because she wouldn't show me his face. 'Is he OK, Mum?' I whispered, very gently touching the tuft of hair. It felt so soft. I could feel the baby's warm pink scalp, so small, so delicate.

'Dixie,' said Mum, like she was about to say something serious.

I looked up at her, my heart pounding. I decided I was going to love my new little brother no matter what.

'Did he get born too soon, Mum?' I asked, patting the blue bundle.

'Well, maybe I got my calculations wrong, darling. I got a lot of things wrong.'

'Mum!' Rochelle came hurtling down the path, screeching her head off.

'Ssh, Rochelle. He's asleep. Don't wake little Sundance. Is that his name still, Mum?'

Mum swallowed. Clutching the baby with one hand, she ran her fingers through her hair, tugging at it. It was as if she was tugging her face too, lighting up her eyes, making her mouth curl up into a big smile.

'Of course he's Sundance, darling,' said Mum. She

peeled back a corner of the blanket, showing us our little brother's face.

'Oh Mum!' I said, nearly in tears. 'Oh Mum, he's lovely!'

'He's so *sweet*!' said Rochelle. 'Look at his little nose and his tiny mouth! Oh, bless him.'

Mum still looked worried, but she rocked baby Sundance proudly. 'Yeah, bless him,' she said softly, and she bent and kissed his little tufty head.

Then Jude and Martine came running out the house too, and everyone circled Mum and kissed little Sundance. We went indoors and Mum sighed at all the furniture still crammed willy nilly in the living room. She collapsed on her mattress, the baby still swaddled in the blanket, clutched tightly in her arms.

'Was it really awful having him, Mum?' Martine asked.

'Well, it was no picnic, darling, put it that way,' said Mum.

'What time was he born?'

'One o'clock this morning.'

'Are you going to do his star chart, Mum?' I asked.

Mum had done all of ours, writing our fortunes in fancy italic writing and putting moons and stars all round the borders, and a clock at the top with the exact time of our birth and little pink baby-girl cherubs on either side.

'His star chart?' said Mum, looking dazed.

'Mum, are you all right?' said Jude, sitting down beside her. 'How come they let you out of hospital already? I thought you were meant to stay in for twenty-four hours?'

'Well, I discharged myself. I didn't fancy staying in there any longer than necessary, not when I needed to get back to you girls. And where's whatshisface? Did he clear off and leave you all by yourselves?'

'He's coming back this morning, Mum, he promised,' I said.

'Yeah, to take us to the hospital, but obviously we don't need him to do that now. Have you got his number, Mum? We'll put him off,' said Martine.

'No! I want to see him!' I said.

'Oh God, Dixie, you're so *sad*. Imagine getting fond of a geeky old twit like that,' said Rochelle, sitting the other side of Mum. 'Can I give him a cuddle, Mum?'

'No, no, leave him be, lovie. I'm hoping he'll nod off to sleep,' said Mum. 'We need to sweet-talk old Bruce back again, Martine. We've got all sorts of baby stuff to get, and I'm not up to running around much at the moment. Plus we've got to get all the furniture shifted.'

'He's got a bad back, Mum,' I said.

'Yeah, so's every fellow I've ever met, when they want to get out of a bit of hard work,' said Mum. 'Pathetic, the lot of them. They should try having the babies, that'd teach them. OK, who's going to make me a nice cup of tea? That hospital cuppa was stewed to death. I need to keep up my liquids if I'm feeding little Sundance.'

'Oh yuck, Mum! Are you really going to feed him yourself? That's so, like, *animal*,' said Rochelle. 'Aren't you scared it'll spoil your figure?'

'Well, I've done it four times over and everything's bobbed back into place – or thereabouts,' said Mum, patting herself.

Her chest was impressively big now but her tummy was much flatter, nearly back to normal. She looked really really tired, though. Her face was so pale, and she had great dark smudges under her eyes. Her hair was all tangled and greasy, hanging lankly about her shoulders.

'Shall I wash your hair for you, Mum?' I said.

'I could run you a bath. We've got lots of hot water. We got the electrics working. If there's any trouble I know how to fix it,' said Jude.

'Can I bath the baby, Mum? Oh please, let me,' said Rochelle. 'Give him here!'

'No, no, no!' said Mum. She said it so fiercely we all jumped and baby Sundance got startled, his little fists flying in the air. He wailed, and Mum rocked him in her arms.

'Ssh, ssh! There now, baby,' she murmured into his tiny red ear.

'Mum?' said Rochelle. 'Mum, I promise I'll be ever so careful with him.'

'I know, I know, but he's not a toy, sweetheart.'

'You let me bath Dixie when she was tiny.'

'I bet you banged my head on the bath!'

'I've bathed all of you,' said Martine on her way out to make the tea. 'Don't worry, Mum, I'll see to him. While I'm still here.'

'No, not just yet, Martine,' said Mum. She took a deep breath. 'Listen, girls, it's hard to explain, like, but we're still bonding, Sundance and me. *I* want to take care of him for the next few days, all right? I don't want any of you bathing him, dressing him up, changing his nappies—'

'Like we'd *want* to change his nappies?' said Jude, pulling a face. 'Mum, you look done in.' She put her hand on Mum's forehead. 'You're burning up. I don't think you should have come out of hospital so soon. When Bruce comes how's about we get him to run you back to the maternity ward, just so they can check you out?'

'No way,' Mum snapped. 'Will you girls quit fussing! All I want is my cup of tea.'

'Here you are, Mum,' said Martine, bringing it in from the kitchen.

Mum drank it down in three gulps and then lay back on her pillow, clutching Sundance. He was nodding off to sleep, his delicate eyelids drooping. Mum nuzzled him close, and in a minute she was asleep too.

The four of us stood watching, still a little awed, like shepherds in a Nativity painting. It seemed so weird that yesterday we'd just been Mum and us four girls. Now this new baby brother had changed everything.

'That's my little brother Sundance,' I whispered to Bluebell.

'And that's my brain-dead sister Dixie who still plays with cuddly toys,' Rochelle said, sighing.

'Ssh! Let's go in the kitchen. We don't want to wake them,' said Martine. 'Come on, we'll all have some tea.'

'Is she *really* going to call him Sundance?' Jude whispered. 'She's so hot, I'm sure she's got a fever. What's childbed fever? Do you think she's got it?'

'Of course not. Shut up, Jude. Come *on*,' said Martine.

We went and huddled in the kitchen. We'd got our own table and chairs in there but it didn't feel like our kitchen at all. The sink was clean now but none of us wanted to go near it. The floor was all stained and dirty, with half of the floor tiles cracked or missing.

I curled my legs up so my bare feet wouldn't touch it. I'd lost one of yesterday's socks in the messy sitting room and I didn't know where my clean ones were. I decided to go without. My trainers rubbed my feet so I left them off too.

I flew Bluebell round and round. She ended up perching on my big toe, gripping it with her wiry little claws.

'Do you *have* to sit like that, Dixie?' said Rochelle. 'Your feet are filthy. This whole house is a tip. Mum's mad bringing us here.'

'I'll say,' said Martine.

'Don't you *ever* stop moaning?' said Jude. 'We'll just have to get this house sorted, that's all.'

'Well don't look at me,' said Rochelle. 'I'm the one that did all the bogging scrubbing. I'm sick of it. I'm next to the youngest, so it's not fair I have to do all the hard work.'

'Not any more,' I said. 'You're in the middle now. Martine and Jude, then you – piggy in the middle! – then me, then Sundance. I'm not the baby any more. He is.'

'Yeah, and I bet he's a lot more clued up than you are already, Dixie. He's sweet, isn't he? So little.'

'I think he looks *big*,' said Martine, sipping at her tea. She pulled a face. 'Think of the size of his head and how it must hurt coming *out*.'

'Don't! Still, Mum's all right now,' said Rochelle.

'No she's not,' said Jude.

'Yeah, well, she's tired, obviously, but she'll be OK when she's had a good sleep,' said Rochelle.

'She looks awful. And she's acting weird,' said Martine. 'All that fuss about us not touching the baby, like we're going to hurt him. What's she on about, all this bonding lark?'

'She did go a bit funny when Dixie was born, remember?' said Jude. 'But then Dixie was in hospital for ages and Mum had to keep trailing backwards and forwards to visit her.'

'And she was still grieving for my dad. She got dead

depressed, she told me,' said Rochelle, nodding importantly.

'I hope she's not getting depressed now,' said Jude.

'*I'm* depressed, stuck here when I want to be back home with Tony,' said Martine.

Jude looked at her. 'Are you really going to walk out on Mum and all of us?' she said.

'I'm not going right this minute. But soon. I've got my own life to lead, Jude. I want to be with Tony.'

'How come he comes before us?'

'Because I love him,' said Martine.

'More than you love Mum and us?'

'Yeah, well, it's different. Look, one day you'll understand,' said Martine.

'*I* understand,' said Rochelle. 'I can't wait – though I wouldn't ever fancy a boy-next-door type like Tony. There's no need to shove me, Martine, he literally *is* the boy next door. No, I want some guy who's really good looking and dynamic and dead sexy.'

'Like that guy with the earring!' said Jude in disgust.

'Well, why not?' said Rochelle. 'I think he was pretty fit.'

'Yeah, fit to take you round the back of the house and mess around with you to show off to all his mates,' said Jude.

'Look, who are you to judge? You don't like boys. I do.'

'He's not a boy, he's a big lout – and you're just a silly little girl,' said Jude.

Rochelle shook her head pityingly, looking at Martine. 'She doesn't have a clue, does she?'

'I don't know,' said Martine, shifting uneasily. 'Maybe you should be careful, Rochelle. Jude's right, you're only a kid. You don't know what you're doing.'

Rochelle flushed. 'Don't you start ganging up on me

too, it's not fair.' She scrabbled in the empty biscuit packet, licking her fingers to get the last of the crumbs. 'I'm still starving. Why can't we have some proper breakfast? And what are we going to have for lunch?'

'Oh dear me, let's all go and ask cook what she's conjured up,' said Jude sarcastically.

I pretended in my head that we really did have a cook – a lovely cheery lady with a red beaming face. She let me lick her cake bowl and called me fond foodie nicknames like Pancake and Cherry Bun. I daydreamed we had lots of servants, a kind chauffeur who whizzed us to the shops and the seaside and all the amusement parks in a big white limo long enough for all us Diamond girls to fit inside.

We were very very rich and we lived in a huge black and white house and we all had our own bedrooms and Bluebell had her own aviary with lots of other budgies, but she always stayed my absolute favourite. I wondered about Bruce and whether he could come and live with us too. Maybe he'd just come and visit, seeing he was my uncle . . .

Then I heard a car door slam outside. It was the real Bruce come visiting! I rushed to the door, worried that the others might get there first and tell him to go away. He was looking anxious, hitching his glasses up and down, with a bulging carrier bag in one hand and a big bouquet of roses and lilies and freesias in the other.

He smiled when he saw me and handed me the bouquet with a flourish. 'Flowers for you, madam,' he said. 'Well, they're actually for you to take to your mum. But you can have a freesia just for you. Here, don't they smell pretty?' He pulled out a little lilac freesia and tucked it in my hair, behind my ear.

'You're all right then, you and your sisters? I was so worried about you stuck here all by yourselves. Martina did stay, didn't she?'

'Yes, we were fine,' I said, patting my flowery hair and then peering in his carrier bag. 'Wow, you've got those flaky roll thingies. And orange juice! Is this all *your* breakfast, Uncle Bruce?'

'Ha ha, as if I'm going to eat a dozen croissants all by myself! No, they're for you and your sisters. Then when you've had your fill we'll see about getting you all to the hospital to see how your mum's getting on.'

'We don't have to go to the hospital, Uncle Bruce. Mum's back already! Come and see.'

I tugged his arm and pulled him indoors. He dumped his bag and the bouquet in the hall and let me pull him towards the crammed living room.

'She's still asleep, don't go in!' Jude hissed.

'Just let him peep at the baby,' I said.

'The baby's nothing to do with him,' said Martine.

'Too right,' said Bruce.

I went on pulling, wanting to show off to him. I crept round the door. I expected Mum to be lying back on the pillow, the duvet up under her chin, but she was sitting up, cradling the baby in her arms. She was crying.

'Mum! Oh Mum, are you in pain?'

'Ssh! No, no, I'm fine, I'm just – over-emotional,' Mum sniffed, wiping her eyes with the silky corner of the baby's blanket.

'You should still be in hospital,' said Bruce.

'Who asked your opinion?' Mum said rudely. 'I had

115

to get back to my girls, didn't I, seeing as you scarpered?'

'Look, they're not *my* responsibility – even though I've come all the way back today and I've got breakfast *and* lunch and tea stuff, and even disposable nappies for the baby. I didn't know what kind to get. Did you have your little boy?'

Mum clutched Sundance tightly. 'Of course.'

'You look a bit rough, if you don't mind my saying so,' said Bruce.

'I do mind! Look, you be Mr Good-Guy and fix the kids something to eat and drink. I want a bit of peace to feed the baby and get him changed. Dixie, where's the box with all the baby things?'

I scrabbled at the hundred and one cardboard boxes all round the living room until I found the right one, crammed with little blue outfits. I fingered the little sleeping suits, making them kick their legs up and down as if they had tiny dancing babies inside them.

'They're all so sweet, Mum. Can Sundance wear these weeny stretchy dungarees? Look, there's a sun embroidered on the front – they're perfect.'

'OK, OK – and find me the little yellow and blue stripy top that goes with it.'

'Let me dress him, Mum, please!'

'No! I told you, *I'm* doing it. I'm doing everything for him. Off you go now.'

'Can't I even watch?'

'No you can't. You go and make yourself useful in the kitchen. He's *my* little boy.'

'He's *my* little baby brother,' I said, edging up to the bed. 'Can I just give him a kiss, Mum?'

'Go on then,' said Mum, sighing. 'But don't go poking at him with that damn budgie, OK?'

I gave Sundance a kiss on his little wrinkled forehead. He was very pink in the face.

'He's hot in that blanket. It can't be much fun for him, all bundled up. Can't he have a little kick without it?'

'You leave him be. I'm the one who knows all about babies,' said Mum, but she suddenly started crying again. 'I'm the one who knows beggar all about anything,' she wailed.

'Don't cry, Mum! Shall I get Jude or Martine?'

'No, just leave me be. Take no notice. You always get weepy just after having a baby. Nothing to worry about,' said Mum.

I couldn't help worrying.

I went into the kitchen and ate part of a croissant, sucking at the end, pretending it was a cigar. Then I stuck it under my nose like a moustache.

'You're a caution, Dixie,' said Bruce.

'Stop encouraging her. Don't play with your food, Dixie,' said Martine.

'Yuck, imagine eating that croissant with Dixie's snot dribbled all over it,' said Rochelle.

'I'm not the slightest bit snotty,' I said, but I went off the idea of eating it all the same.

Jude wanted to take Mum a croissant but Mum yelled at her to go away.

'She's got a mouth on her, your mum,' said Bruce.

'Well, she's not feeling too great, is she?' said Martine. '*You* try having a baby.'

'I'm never ever having babies,' I said.

'Me neither,' said Jude, eating Mum's croissant herself.

117

'Nor me. It mucks up your figure, makes you go all saggy,' said Rochelle, posing to show off her own perfect figure. 'What about you, Martine? You're Mum's last hope of being a granny.'

'Don't look at me!' Martine said fiercely.

'Don't you and Tony want to have little Martys and Tones?' said Jude.

'I wish you'd just shut *up* about it,' said Martine.

'I'm sick of people telling me to shut up and clear off,' said Jude. 'OK, I will. I'm going for a mooch around.'

'No, you can't! You've got to help get this dump organized,' said Martine.

'Watch me,' said Jude. She walked out of the kitchen, down the hall and out the front door.

'That's just typical of her,' said Martine. 'She's the strongest. How are we going to get all that furniture shifted without her?' She was looking at Bruce.

'I can't, Martina,' said Bruce. 'My back's really twingeing from yesterday. If I put it out I'll be flat on my back for a week, when I've got to drive up town for my flowers, keep the shop open, manage the deliveries. I can't risk it.'

'Well, we'll just manage ourselves, you and me, Rochelle,' said Martine.

'No way! If Jude can skive off, so can I,' said Rochelle, reaching for her denim jacket. 'I'm going out too.'

'No you're not.'

'If Jude can, I can.'

'Jude's older. She can look after herself. You're staying here. Rochelle.'

'You can't boss me about. You're not my mother,' Rochelle said. 'I'm just going down the road, that's all. OK?'

'No, it's not OK.'

'Well, tough,' said Rochelle, and she ran for it.

Martine ran after her, but gave up when Rochelle was out the door. 'It's not *fair*,' she said, nearly in tears. 'I get my whole life messed up and come here to help out and find I get left doing everything, just because I'm the eldest.'

'I hope you're not going to clear off too,' said Bruce. 'I can't stay too long, you know. You can't leave little Dixie in charge.'

'I'm *not* little!' I said.

'Oh yes, look at you growing, practically towering above me,' said Bruce, peering at an imaginary giraffe-necked Dixie.

'I know I'm small, but I'm not a baby,' I said firmly.

Maybe this wasn't a wise thing to say.

'OK, you can make yourself useful,' said Martine. She braved Mum in the living room and humped several boxes of pots and packets and china into the kitchen. 'You can scrub out all the cupboards and put our stuff in them. I'll make a start cleaning upstairs.'

Martine swished off with a broom and scrubbing brush, looking martyred. We heard her phoning Tony as she went upstairs: 'Yes, Mum's had the baby . . . Sure, they're both fine . . . Well, Mum's a bit whacked, obviously, so I'm having to do *everything* at the moment. The girls are no help whatsoever.'

'Cheek!' I said.

'Yes, double cheek! She didn't even mention me,' said Bruce.

'Exactly. We wouldn't have any light or hot water or breakfast without you, Uncle Bruce. We wouldn't even *be* here.'

'Ah. Maybe that's why she's so cross with me. Anyway,

I didn't come back here for her. Or your sisters. Or your mum.' He smiled at me, forgetting to hide his funny teeth. I smiled back.

'It's because you're my dad's mate, isn't it, Uncle Bruce?'

'I don't know about that. It's more this uncle lark. I'm getting to like the idea of you as my token niece, little Dixie.' Bruce sighed and stretched. 'But I'm also here to help out, so I'd better get on.'

'You mustn't muck up your back, Uncle Bruce.'

'No, I can't do any lifting, darling. I thought I'd busy myself checking out the whole house, making sure your washing machine's plumbed in properly, testing the cooker – boring stuff like that.'

'You are a total star, Uncle Bruce,' I said.

'Twinkle, twinkle,' he said, waggling his eyebrows at me, his glasses sliding down his nose.

I giggled and then sat down beside the boxes, poking about amongst the china and cutlery. I didn't know where to start. I got out all our different cups and lined them up on the floor, as if they were standing in a queue. Then I found the teapot and turned it into an elephant. The cup children took turns riding on its back, rewarding it with a sugar lump down its spouty trunk.

Bruce decided he needed his tool box and stepped backwards. He crushed a child and very nearly killed the elephant too. We picked up the pieces together.

'Maybe you'd better get the cupboards cleaned up, like your sister said. Then you can put all this china safely away,' Bruce said.

He stood me on a chair with a wet J-cloth and a tin of Vim. I scattered the white powder over the black grime and mouldy crumbs. I gave the shelf a little rub. Nothing much happened. It was like powdering a very dirty face.

'You need to give it a bit of elbow grease,' said Bruce, showing me how to scrub vigorously.

I tried to copy him but I couldn't reach comfortably. It made my arm ache and I rattled around on the chair so much I nearly skidded right off.

'Careful, Dixie! I don't think you're very safe wobbling about on that chair. Maybe you've done enough work now. I should go and have a little play in the garden.'

'But what about the cupboard?'

'I'll give it a going over for you when I'm done here,' said Bruce. 'Don't worry, we'll get this house shipshape in no time.'

'Shipshape?'

'Everything running smoothly.'

I thought about it. Things had never run smoothly, not even in any of our old flats. If we were in a ship it was always an old leaky one, and we were tossing up and down in a storm. Still, as long as we were all clinging together, safe inside the ship, that was all that mattered.

10

I skipped off out of the door and into the jungle. Bluebell came fluttering out of my Vim-crusted cuff and swooped up and down in delight. She sang a wild Australian song (I cheeped 'Waltzing Matilda') her wings spread wide.

'Don't fly too far, Bluebell. We're going to go and see Mary.'

We trekked through the jungle together and then I hauled myself up onto the Great Wall of China. There was Mary on the swing, in a blue-check dress, white ribbons fluttering on her plaits, lacy white socks and navy patent button shoes. She was peering round. When she saw my head above the wall she smiled and jumped off the swing, running towards the gate.

I clambered over the wall and ran across the alley.

'Hi, Mary!' I said.

'Hello, Dixie. I've been looking and looking for you! Do you want to come in and have a swing?'

'Yes please! But I don't want to get you into trouble.

You said your mum won't let you have friends round to play.'

'Mummy's out at church. Daddy's here, but he's still in bed. So you can come for a bit, but we have to be quiet.'

'As a mouse!' I said. I twitched my nose and went '*Squeak-squeak.*'

Mary giggled. She seemed happy to see me, but her eyes were red and sore, and her voice was husky, as if she'd been crying again.

'Are you all right, Mary?' I asked, wriggling onto the swing.

'I'm fine,' she said, though she didn't look fine at all.

She was as pin-neat as ever, her plaits pulled so tightly back behind her ears she could barely blink. There was something the matter with her hands. She had them curled into tight fists.

'Have you been crying?'

'No,' said Mary nervously.

'It's OK. I cry lots. We *all* cry in our family. My mum says it's a wonder we're not sloshing about ankle-deep in tears. Hey, Mary, guess what! Mum's had her baby. I've got my baby brother. He's so sweet. Maybe I can bring him round to see you soon. Do you like babies?'

Mary didn't look sure.

'I've got a baby boy,' she said surprisingly.

'No you haven't!'

'I'll show you.'

She ran off, her feet stiff in her patent shoes. She went in her back door and came out a minute later pushing a baby buggy almost as big as a real one. There was a peachy-skinned plastic baby doll sitting up in it, a fixed grin on his face.

'Oh wow! He's beautiful,' I said, though that grin looked a bit scary, and I didn't like the way his rigid pink fingers were reaching out, ready to grab at me.

Mary didn't seem too relaxed with him either. She pushed the buggy half-heartedly, and didn't touch the baby, even when he tipped over to one side.

'What's his name?' I said.

'Baby,' said Mary.

'Baby what?'

'Shall I call him Sundance too?'

'You could call him Butch, then they could maybe be friends. Do you take Baby Butch to bed with you?'

'Oh no. I'm not allowed. I might mess him up. I take my teddy to bed with me. I like my teddy best, even though he's old.'

'Old toys are much nicer.'

'Like Bluebell?'

'*I'm not a toy, I'm a bird,*' Bluebell chirruped. '*I like your garden, Mary. I think I might make a little holiday nest here.*'

I flew Bluebell round and round, looking for twigs. There were none on the velvet-green grass, so I had to snap some off the hedge. Mary looked tense. She didn't help me. Her fingers were still curled inside her palms.

I tried to bundle my little twigs together but they kept collapsing. 'I think birds must have secret gluepots,' I said. 'Oh, blow this for a game of soldiers. Hey, look, we could turn all the twigs into little soldiers and play armies.'

'I don't know how to play armies.'

'We'll just make it up.'

'I don't know *how*,' said Mary, sounding upset.

'OK, OK. Let's play families. Mother twig, father twig, lots of little kiddie twigs, yeah?'

'Yeah,' said Mary, but she kept her hands in little clenched fists, not taking hold of any of the twigs.

'Just watch me then,' I said. I took hold of a twig. 'Hello, hello, hello, I'm little Tilly Twig and I'm going to dance a jig,' I said, making her dance in front of Mary's face.

Mary smiled.

'You make little Tommy Twig dance with her,' I said.

'No, you do him too,' said Mary.

So I made Tilly and Tommy twirl for a minute.

'Find new little baby Titchy Twiglet and make him dance.'

'Babies can't dance,' said Mary.

'OK, he wants to crawl. Yeah, he can be crawling around and Tilly and Tommy keep falling over him.'

'You make him crawl, Dixie,' said Mary.

'You'll have to help. I haven't got three hands. There!' I snapped a tiny piece off a twig. 'Look, here he is, tiny Titchy. Isn't he sweet? Oh, he's crawling away from me. Catch him, Mary!'

I threw the little piece of twig. Mary obediently cupped her hands to catch him. The tips of her fingers were bright pink and sore, each small nail cut right back to the quick.

'Mary! Your nails!'

She dropped the little twig and curved her hands into fists again.

'Whatever did you *do* to them? Did you try and cut them yourself?'

'Yes,' Mary whispered, head bent.

'But it must have hurt awfully. Why did you *do* it? Why didn't you get your mum to cut your nails?'

Mary said nothing.

'Mary? Did your mum cut your nails?'

Mary said nothing. Her chin was on her chest, her white parting painfully obvious, raked into her head. I put my arms round her.

'She did, didn't she?' I said.

Mary started crying. 'They were dirty nails and Mummy said I'm a bad, dirty girl and I can't have nails like a little animal even though I act like one. So she cut them off,' Mary sobbed in a rush.

'Why didn't you run away?'

'She had me tight between her legs so I couldn't.'

'But it must be so so so sore.'

'I couldn't stop crying and that made Mummy cross.'

'Did she smack you?'

'You always get a hard smack if you cry.'

'My mum doesn't ever smack me.'

'My mummy smacks me lots. I deserve it because I'm bad,' said Mary.

'That's rubbish. You're not a *bit* bad. I don't know how your mum would cope with Rochelle. Or Jude. Or Martine. What about your dad – does he smack you too?'

'No, he gives me cuddles. But he says I've got to try not to be so naughty because it upsets Mummy.'

'But you're *not* naughty.'

'I am. I do really dirty things,' Mary said hoarsely.

'Like what?'

'I pick my nose. I scratch myself. And sometimes I don't get to the toilet in time.'

'You and everyone else in the entire world!'

126

'I get my clothes dirty.'

'You're the cleanest little girl I've ever seen. You always look like you've just jumped out of your bath. Heaps and heaps and heaps cleaner than me.'

'Mummy says I'm still dirty. Sometimes the dirt doesn't show but she can see it. Or the dirt's inside me and I have to take medicine to get it out.'

I stared at her. 'Your mum's nuts,' I said.

Mary looked startled. 'No she's not!'

'She's worse than nuts. She's cruel,' I said, gently picking up one of Mary's tiny hands. I blew softly on her poor pink fingers. 'I'm blowing fairy dust on them. That'll make them get better quickly.'

'They're better already,' Mary fibbed politely.

'I'm going to tell my mum what your mum did,' I said.

'No! No, you mustn't! Please please please don't tell, Dixie,' Mary begged. She seized hold of me, even though it must have really hurt her fingers. 'Promise you won't tell. I told a girl in my class at school and her mum said something to my mummy. She said it was all a mistake and I was just telling stories. But then when I got home she got the scissors out of her sewing basket and said she'd cut off my tongue if I ever told tales again.'

'She wouldn't *really* cut off your tongue, Mary,' I said. But what sort of mother could cut her little girl's nails right back so savagely? How could I be sure?

'Will you promise you won't tell? If you don't keep your promise I'll drop down dead and die!'

'I promise! But you won't drop down dead and die, Mary. Don't say that, it's horrible. Your mum's horrible.'

'No, she's not. She's the loveliest nicest kindest mummy in the whole world,' said Mary.

She'd used these exact words before. She'd obviously been taught to say it.

I didn't know what to do when I went back to my own house. I wanted to cry when I thought of Mary being hurt. I knew I should tell someone, but I'd promised. I knew it was silly, but I could see myself telling Mum and then Mary keeling over and dying right in front of me.

'You look a bit doleful, Dixie,' said Uncle Bruce, when I went into the kitchen. 'What's up? You can tell your Uncle Bruce, can't you?'

'No, I can't,' I said, sighing.

I heard someone moving around in the living room. 'That's Mum!' I said.

I went running in to see her. Mum was hanging onto a pile of cardboard boxes, her face grey. Sundance was clutched tight in her other arm.

'Mum?'

'I'm OK, Dixie,' she mumbled.

'You're not. I think you'd better lie down again.'

'No, no. Look, I've got to go upstairs to the bathroom, sort myself out. Will you help me, lovie?'

'OK, Mum. Here, lean on me. Why don't you let me take Sundance?'

'No, I've got him,' said Mum.

He was awake now, his eyes wide open. They were a beautiful clear blue, though the lashes were black, like his soft tufty hair. He had lovely little arched eyebrows too, each tiny hair perfect. It seemed astonishing that he'd been forming in Mum's tummy all this time, all the delicate differences – soft skin, shiny eyes, downy hair.

'Don't go all moony on me, Dixie! I'm in a bad way, bleeding,' Mum said impatiently.

'Oh Mum! You've got to go to the hospital!'

'No, love, it's natural. It happens after you have a baby. I'll be all right.'

'Uncle Bruce could take you, just to make sure.'

'No! I'm not going back to that hospital. I'll be fine. I just need a bath. Now, let me lean on you.'

Mum shuffled along, Sundance still clutched tight. Halfway up the stairs Martine heard us and came running.

'Come on, Mum. I'll help you,' she said, dropping her brush and pail. 'I've just cleaned the bathroom.'

'Thanks, darling,' Mum said weakly. She leaned against the wall. 'Oh God, everything's spinning.'

'Look, I'll help you into the bath, come on,' said Martine. 'Dixie, take the baby.'

'No! No, I must keep him,' said Mum, swaying.

'Yeah, right, and you're going to drop him on his head any minute, so how daft is that!' said Martine. 'Dixie, take him!'

I hooked little Sundance out of Mum's arms. She staggered into the bathroom with Martine. I heard them murmuring together, the bath running.

I looked down at my little brother. He was surprisingly heavy for such a tiny baby. He was warm and wriggly . . . and very very wet. He'd wee'd right through his nappy and his little blue sleeping suit. Even his shawl had started to get soggy.

He started snuffling, mewing softly like a kitten.

'It's uncomfy, isn't it?' I whispered. 'I'm going to get you sorted out, little brother.'

I carried him very carefully downstairs, checking every step as I went. I could feel Sundance tensing inside his shawl. 'Don't worry, darling,' I whispered. 'I'm your big sister Dixie. I'll look after you.'

I carried him into the crowded living room and put him down very gently on Mum's mattress. I spread a towel under him, just in case, and found the pack of nappies and a box of tissues and some baby cream.

'There!' I said, proud of myself. 'OK, little boy, we'll soon have you clean and dry and happy.'

I unravelled the shawl carefully, as if I was unwrapping a very special present. Sundance kicked his damp legs happily. I caught hold of his dear little feet.

'I think you really are going to be a footballer,' I said. I unpopped his sleeping suit and peeled his little legs free.

'There! That's good, isn't it? Oh, you're so cute,' I crooned. 'Now, we've just got to get your gungy wet nappy off. Hold still a minute, there's a good boy.'

I tugged the plastic ties undone and cautiously pulled the nappy away from his bottom.

Then I stared.

I looked for Sundance's little willy.

He didn't have one.

He wasn't a baby boy.

He was quite unmistakably a little girl.

11

I didn't know what to do. I kept blinking at Sundance's little bare bottom, hoping it would rearrange itself in front of my eyes.

Sundance was a boy. Mum had known right from the start. She'd consulted her star charts, read the tarot, dangled rings above her stomach, gazed into her crystal ball. Jude had scoffed – but then Mum went to the hospital for her scan and they confirmed it. She was definitely having a baby boy.

Mum had bought a pair of little blue booties that very day. She'd stuck them on the ends of her fingers and made them dance up and down her tummy. She'd had a little baby boy. She'd *said* so. She'd called him her little son.

Perhaps the hospital had made a terrible mistake and mixed up the babies. Maybe my little brother Sundance had been whisked away by the wrong mother, leaving this dark little changeling girl by mistake.

'Who are you?' I whispered to the baby.

She didn't know. She kicked her tiny legs, her little feet arching, her toes so weeny, each tipped by the tiniest slither of nail. Her bottom looked very bare indeed as she lay there, flat on her back.

I got her a clean nappy and covered her up with it. I thought about finding her another sleeping suit as the legs were damp, but then Mum would know for sure that I'd undressed her.

I bundled her back into the damp leggings and wrapped the shawl round her. She didn't seem to mind. I looked at the wet nappy, not knowing what to do with it. I couldn't let Mum find it.

I gazed around the crowded room desperately. Rochelle's fancy white dressing table with the little gilt handles was right in front of me. She'd seen it at a car boot sale and nagged Mum rotten until she bought it for her. I opened the top drawer quickly and shoved the sopping nappy inside. Then I picked the baby up and held her against my thudding heart.

I didn't know what to do. I wished Jude hadn't sloped off. I heard Bruce whistling in the kitchen and wondered about telling him, but it seemed too extraordinary, too personal, too strange. I was already starting to wonder if I could possibly have been mistaken. I didn't know much about babies after all. I'd never seen a baby boy naked. Maybe they had very tiny willies at that age and I'd simply not noticed it. I wanted to undress the baby all over again to have another look but I could hear Martine murmuring above my head and I wasn't sure how long they were going to be.

I sat cross-legged on the mattress, holding the baby in my arms. 'Are you my *sister*?'

She looked at me with her strange blue eyes as if she understood, but couldn't tell me one way or the other. Then Mum and Martine came back, Mum a little pinker now and wearing her rose-red silky nightie and black embroidered kimono, trying to look pretty. Her hair was wet and tied back in a ponytail. She usually looked very young when she tied her hair back – schoolgirly, like our sister instead of our mum. But today she looked like an old lady.

She looked at me anxiously. 'Is Sundance asleep?'

'Nearly.'

'I'll feed him in a little while, get him changed, and then we can both have a nap,' said Mum. 'Give him here, Dixie. You two girls run along. Thank you, Martine. I feel a new woman now.'

We settled Mum down on the mattress and then went out into the hall together. Martine was shaking.

'I had to bath her,' she said. 'She's in such a *state*. Her tummy's all saggy and flabby still. I thought they just snapped back into place. And her boobs are all swollen. They look awful. *She* looks awful.'

'No she doesn't,' I said, because it seemed so mean to agree.

Martine was holding her own flat stomach, shaking her head. 'It's so *stupid*. Why does it have to be so messy and painful? Why can't we be like kangaroos and have babies the size of baked beans that just crawl up into a pocket in our stomachs?'

We both thought about it – and shuddered.

'Yuck,' I said.

'Yes, OK, *bad* idea,' said Martine, giggling, though she looked as if she might start crying instead.

I swallowed. 'Martine. Martine, I've got to tell you something,' I said.

'Not now, Dixie. I need to phone Tony.'

'But it's *important*. It's about the baby.'

'Yeah, well, tell me later, Dixie,' said Martine, running up the stairs, dialling as she went.

I was about to trail after her when there was a knock at the door. I went rushing to open it, hoping it was Jude.

It was Rochelle, jumping up and down in her suede heels, sparkling like a real diamond.

'Guess what, guess what, guess what!' she said.

'*You'll* never guess,' I said. 'Rochelle, come here.' I seized her by the arm and marched her past the living room, making *ssh!* gestures.

'Ah. Yes. Better not tell Mum. You won't tell, Dixie, will you?' Rochelle whispered urgently.

'Tell what?'

'I've got a boyfriend!' said Rochelle, and she twirled around, shaking her head wildly so that her long blonde curls flew up in a glorious golden halo.

'You what? Yeah, like you've stared at some boy and he's waved at you,' I said.

'No, really. I've got a date. Tonight. A *real* date, outside McDonald's. We'll maybe go for a drink later.'

'In a *pub*? As if they'd let you in – you're only twelve!'

'I'm nearly thirteen. He thinks I'm a bit older anyway.'

'How old is he?'

'Sixteen,' said Rochelle proudly.

'You're mad! You can't go out with a sixteen-year-old.' I stood still, halfway up the stairs. 'It's not that guy who had the fight with Jude?'

'Not the big fat one! No, the really cool guy with the

scarf and the earring. He likes me, Dixie, he really does. He says I'm much prettier than any of the other girls on the Planet Estate. He thinks that's why Jude made such a fool of herself. He says she must be jealous of me, seeing as I'm the pretty one.'

'Stop showing off!' I said.

'Look, *I* didn't say I was pretty. Ryan did.'

'That's his name?'

'Yes, isn't it great? Ryan and Rochelle. We sound like a couple already. And if you count up the letters in our names and play Love, Like, Hate, Adore, then we both come out Adore – how about that!'

'You can't adore him, you don't even *know* him yet.'

'Well, I'm going to get to know him properly tonight, aren't I?'

'You're not *really* going on a date with him?'

'I am, I am, I am! Has Brucie Weirdo got the washing machine working? I need to wash my best jeans.'

'Mum will go mad if she finds out.'

'Well, she won't find out, will she? Unless you tell her. And you're not going to tell, are you, Dixie?' Rochelle caught hold of me, her hands digging into my shoulders like big bird claws. 'You're not to tell Martine either. You're especially not going to tell Jude. Because if you do I'm going to take that stupid stuffed budgie and tear its head off, OK?'

Rochelle gave me a little shake to show she really meant it. I knew she'd probably tear *my* head off my shoulders too.

She went singing into the living room to find her boxes of clothes. I heard Mum mumbling something crossly, but Rochelle took no notice. She came out nudging a box across the bare floorboards, holding something wrapped in newspaper in one hand. Her arm stuck out stiffly, her face screwed up in disgust.

'Yuck! Dirty nappy alert. What am I going to *do* with it? Here, Dixie.' Rochelle tried to pass it on to me. I put my hands behind my back and dodged, running to Bruce in the kitchen.

If Mum had changed Sundance then she must have *seen* she wasn't a boy. What was she playing at? She was acting like a crazy person.

'You OK, Dixie?' said Bruce. 'Was that Roxanne having a go at you? What was she saying?'

'Oh, nothing much.'

'What is it? Are you *sure* you can't tell your Uncle Bruce. Spit it out, sweetheart.'

I couldn't spit out all the things that were troubling me or he'd be dripping from head to foot. I decided on a minimalist spit.

'Uncle Bruce, what do you do with dirty nappies?' I remembered there was still one hidden in Rochelle's dressing-table drawer. I decided it served her right. 'Shall I throw this down the toilet?'

Bruce stopped tapping pipes and stared at me. 'You must never ever throw them down the toilet, Dixie,' he said firmly. 'I've got enough to do sorting out this house without you blocking up the toilets.'

'So what *do* you do with them?'

'*I* don't know. It's not a problem I'm used to. Ask your sisters.'

'They're all busy,' I said.

Then I heard another knock at the door. 'Jude!' I said joyfully.

I flew to the front door. Then I stopped and stared. Jude had blood all over her face.

'Jude, what's *happened*? Mum! Martine! Uncle Bruce!'

'Shut *up*, Dixie,' said Jude, clapping her hand over my mouth.

'What have you done? You're bleeding!'

'I'm OK. I've just had a little nosebleed, that's all. Quit flapping, I'm fine.' She wiped her nose angrily on the edge of her T-shirt.

'No you're not.' I peered at her furious face. 'It's not just a nosebleed. Did someone hit you?'

'No! I fell over. Stupid of me. Now shut up about it.'

'I won't shut up! You didn't fall over, someone *knocked* you over. Oh Jude, was it that Ryan?'

'Who?'

'The boy Rochelle's nuts about. Oh gosh, I've told! But if he's beaten you up—'

'*No one's* beaten me up. Especially not that idiot with the earring. I could flatten him with one finger.' Jude sniffed contemptuously. Bubbles of blood came out of her nose. I gave a little squeal.

'Are you all right, Dixie?' Bruce called from the kitchen. 'What's the matter?'

'Nothing! You mind your own business,' Jude said fiercely. 'I'm going to wash the blood off.'

'You can't, Rochelle's in the bathroom.'

'Well, she'll have to get *out* of the bathroom because *I* need it,' Jude said thickly.

Bruce came out into the hall. 'Ouch,' he said, looking at Jude. 'Come into the kitchen. We'll put a wet towel on your nose – that'll stop it. Come on, Jade.'

'It's bloody *Jude*,' said Jude.

'Yes, you are bloody, Jude. You're bleeding like a stuck pig and making a mess of your shirt. Come here,' said Bruce. He took hold of her by the wrist and pulled.

I thought she'd sock him straight in his sticky-out teeth. She can't stand anyone pulling her, not even me. She did struggle for a few seconds, but then she gave in and let him steer her into the kitchen. She was shivering now and he patted her gently on the shoulder. He patted me too.

'Cheer up, chickie,' he said to me. 'We'll soon get your sister cleaned up.'

He didn't waste time asking how she'd got a bloody nose. He just fished an old towel out of the kitchen cardboard box, soaked it under the tap and held it firmly against her nose.

'There we are. Put your head back a bit.' He looked down at her right hand. The knuckles were bleeding. 'I think you need something on those knuckles too.'

'Do you think we need to take Jude to hospital, Uncle Bruce?'

'You Diamonds are turning my van into an ambulance service! No, she'll be fine, nothing to fuss about, like she said. We'll have a proper squint at that sore nose once it's stopped bleeding but I don't think she's broken it. I've got a little first aid kit in the van. I'll rustle up some arnica to stop the bruising and a spot of antiseptic for those knuckles. I'm a one-man casualty department.'

He went off to get them while Jude hid her head in the towel.

'Isn't Uncle Bruce magic?' I said.

'Bruce is not our blooming uncle,' Jude mumbled from

underneath the towel. She sounded as if she might be crying, though Jude never cries.

'Does it hurt ever so badly?'

'No, I'm fine, I *said*,' Jude insisted.

When Bruce came back she let him mop up the last of the blood and then gently feel along her nose. He cleaned her hand too. She winced when he rubbed antiseptic into the split knuckles but she didn't complain.

'You're a brave girl,' said Bruce.

'Rubbish,' said Jude. She was still shivering.

'Make us all a cup of tea, Dixie,' said Bruce. 'We'll give Jude lots of sugar for the shock. And me lots of sugar because I'm greedy.'

'I'm not *in* shock,' said Jude.

'You can't help but be in shock when you get beaten up,' said Bruce.

'I *haven't* been beaten up,' said Jude. 'No one ever beats me up. I can look after myself.'

'Yeah?' said Bruce. 'Mmm.'

'Look, all right, these boys had a go at me, but they took me by surprise. I didn't even see them coming. I was going up these steps and they kind of ambushed me. I didn't even know it was happening. They just laid into me. I did hit one of them. He went sprawling.'

'I should say so,' said Bruce, looking at her knuckles.

'I think he just tripped though. But he looked like he'd hurt himself.'

'Never mind him. You're the one that's hurt. A gang of yobs picking on one small girl! I thought I'd made it clear to that thick bunch to lay off all you Diamond girls.'

139

'We don't need you to fight our battles,' Jude said automatically. She paused. 'But thanks. No, this was a new gang, a different one.'

'Did they just start hitting you for nothing, Jude?'

'Well, they made out I was on their territory. They call themselves the Mercury Top Floor Boys – I mean, how sad is that? I laughed and said they were all plonkers and they couldn't stop me going wherever I wanted . . . only they did.'

'Oh Jude, promise you won't ever go there again!' I begged.

'I'll go where I want. We live on Mercury too,' Jude said defiantly.

'You'd better learn to defend yourself then,' said Bruce.

Jude jerked away from him. 'I can fight! I can take on anyone!'

'Jude's famous for fighting,' I said.

'Yes, I can see you could be handy with your fists, girl, but you need to use your whole body.' Bruce stood up straight in his baggy T-shirt and saggy trackies. 'OK, I know I'm not Mr Big Shot Muscleman, but I know what I'm saying.'

'Which is?'

'When you're in a fight situation and you can't back down—'

'I *never* back down.'

'You don't have to meet force with force. You block it. Go on, try to hit me.'

'I don't think that's a good idea, Uncle Bruce,' I said quickly.

'Give it a go, Jade,' said Bruce.

'*Jude!*' said Jude, swinging a punch at him.

Bruce brought his arm up, hand open, and blocked Jude's punch easily.

'Oh,' said Jude, trying not to look impressed. 'Kung fu! I suppose you watch all those Bruce Lee films. Your namesake, eh?'

'I actually took his name,' Bruce said, blushing. 'The greatest guy with the greatest philosophy on life.'

'Yeah, well, I'm not into all that great-guy stuff, thanks,' said Jude, jumping up.

'I practise Wing Chun kung fu – and Wing Chun was a woman,' said Bruce.

'You're kidding!'

'Truly. And because it's the only system devised by a woman it's especially suited to them. And weedy blokes like me. It depends on technique, not power. You're like a coiled spring.'

'Show me,' said Jude, giggling.

'Well, you can't just pick it up in an afternoon, girl. I've been going to classes for years, and I've read stuff, seen lots of videos. It's a whole way of life. Still, I can show you the basic movements.'

Bruce stood in the middle of the kitchen and demonstrated. He should have looked ridiculous, straddling his little legs and waving his skinny arms around in his *Simpsons* T-shirt, but somehow he looked pretty good. He didn't hitch his glasses up and down or grin nervously, hiding his teeth. His face was pure concentration, totally dignified.

'Wow,' said Jude.

I peered at her anxiously, but she wasn't sending him up, she was serious. She tried to copy what Bruce was doing.

'No, no, no. You start like this,' Bruce said. 'OK, the Horse Stance is the basic position. Stand with your legs together. Let your arms dangle by your side, nice and relaxed. Breathe easily. Well, it's meant to be through the nose but yours is a bit sore and stuffed up right now. Just do your best. Empty your mind. Let go of all your thoughts.'

Jude stood obediently, her feet together, arms dangling. I tried to do it too, but I couldn't empty my mind. My thoughts buzzed back and forth like bees. Sundance lay kicking in the middle of my mind, baring her little girl's bottom.

'I changed Sundance's nappy,' I blurted out.

'Yes, yes, well done, Dixie, but shush now, we're concentrating.'

'Dixie doesn't know how to concentrate,' said Jude.

She was wrong. I was concentrating so fiercely on Sundance I couldn't think about anything else, especially this Horse Stance.

I watched them sliding their heels and standing pointy-kneed. Bruce told Jude to imagine trapping a goat between her knees. She didn't giggle. She did her best to copy him. I saw a big brown billy goat between Bruce's knees; a little white woolly kid goat trapped between Jude's. I could smell their strange goaty stink, hear their indignant bleats. They seemed so real, but I knew they weren't there, I was just imagining them.

I clutched Bluebell, stroking her beak for comfort. She fluttered free, fanning her wings to cool my hot face. No. I was *imagining* her circling my head in a whirl of sky-blue. Maybe I was imagining Sundance's lack of little willy . . .

There was only one way to find out. I left Bruce and Jude in their weird Horse Stances and tiptoed into the living room. Mum was lying on the mattress, her dark hair tousled on the pillow. Her eyes were closed.

Sundance was lying beside her, wrapped in the blue blanket. I crept nearer, holding my breath. I got right up to the mattress. Mum still didn't stir. Sundance was sleeping too. I leaned over, hands outstretched. It would only take two seconds to unpop the little legs of the sleeping suit and open up the nappy. I flexed my fingers, willing them to work nimbly.

I grabbed the blue blanket.

'Leave your little brother alone!'

I nearly fell right on top of Sundance and smothered him. Mum propped herself up on her elbows, glaring at me.

'I told you to leave him be, Dixie!' she hissed.

'I'm sorry, Mum.'

'So you should be! Now push off and leave us in peace.'

'Yes, Mum,' I said.

I started crying as I backed out of the room, bumping into all the furniture.

'Oh for Gawd's sake, stop that,' said Mum. '*I* should be the one who's howling. I'm lying here like a beached whale, still all fat and flabby. I've ended up in a rubbish house at the back of beyond with five kids to care for. What am I going to do, eh? What have *you* got to cry about, Dixie Daydream?'

'Nothing,' I said, sobbing harder.

Sundance snuffled and started crying too.

'There! Now you've woken your little brother and he'll want another flipping feed.'

Mum sighed deeply and started unbuttoning her top. She picked Sundance up, still wrapped in the blanket like a swiss roll. She cradled him, his little downy head against her big white breast.

'Who's my greedy little darling?' Mum whispered. 'That's my boy. My thirsty little lad. You'll be a one for the beer when you're older.' Mum looked at me. 'Off you go then, Dixie. I feel all self-conscious with you staring at me like that. Dry your eyes, darling. There's nothing to cry about. You've got a lovely little brother, the most gorgeous boy in all the world.'

'No he's not,' I sobbed.

Mum frowned at me. 'Yes he is! For God's sake, Dixie, you're ten years old. You're surely not *jealous* of your little brother?'

'But he's not my real brother, Mum.'

'*Now* what are you on about?' Mum was so indignant her breasts bounced and Sundance came unlatched. 'Of course he's your real brother. Like Martine and Jude and Rochelle are your real sisters. Never mind about the dads. I'm your mum. I'm his mum. Simple.'

'I *know*, Mum.'

'You're driving me bonkers, Dixie! You know *what*?' Mum asked, trying to start Sundance feeding again. 'Come on, little darling, more drinkies. Don't let your silly sister put you off. We need to build you up, my lad, you're such a tiny little boy.'

I knelt down beside Mum. 'He's not a little boy, Mum. He's a little girl.'

'You what?' said Mum.

'You heard me, Mum. I know. I've seen him. I mean her. Sundance is a girl.'

'Don't be so stupid!' said Mum. 'Look at him. He's a boy. Of course he's a little boy.'

'I don't know why you're *saying* all this, Mum. Let's look at Sundance then. We'll soon see.'

'Get your hands off him!' Mum shouted. She held Sundance so tight he got frightened, and started crying.

'Are you OK in there? Can I get you anything?' Bruce called outside the door. 'Dixie, come in the kitchen with Jude and me and leave your mum alone.'

'In a minute, Uncle Bruce. I'm *helping* Mum.'

We heard him go back to the kitchen. Mum clutched Sundance, rocking backwards and forwards.

'You're a beautiful boy, aren't you, darling? Stupid stupid Dixie! How could you possibly not be a boy, little Sundance?'

'Take the nappy off, Mum.'

'You leave him be!'

'Look, Mum!' I said, scrabbling at Sundance's legs, trying to get hold of the nappy.

'Stop that! I don't want to look. I won't!' said Mum.

'Don't be mad, Mum. You can't pretend Sundance is a boy!'

'I can!'

'But what are you going to do – hide her bum from everyone for ever? That's just crazy. What about the baby clinic? Are you going to dress her in boys' clothes all the time? What about when she starts nursery? They'll take her to the boys' toilets in her little trousers and then what's she going to do? She won't be able to wee standing up.'

'All right, all right, give it a *rest*, Dixie. I know I can't keep her a boy for ever. I just want a few days, that's all. That's not too much to ask, is it? I wanted a boy so much. Every single symbol and sign showed I was having a boy – it was in all the charts, all the readings. I was so *sure*. I wouldn't ever swap you girls, I love you to bits, but you *know* how much I've always wanted a boy.'

'What about the scan, Mum? You said they told you the baby was a boy.'

'They did, they did. Well. I was sure they would have done. I so needed the baby to be a boy I didn't want them to cast any doubts. They're all such know-alls at these hospitals. That's why I came home just now, as soon as I could nip out without them noticing. I didn't want them telling me what to do, talking about my little girl, my baby daughter. I've *got* my daughters. I want a son!' She cradled Sundance, her hand cupped round her small head.

'She's not a son.'

'Let me pretend for a bit, Dixie. Just for a little while, to make me happy. I can't bear it that I got it all wrong. You're my daydream pretender girl. You know what it's like. Not like the others. Don't tell your sisters!'

'But—'

'You can't tell them, Dixie. They'll think I've gone nuts.'

'*I* think you've gone nuts.'

'Martine's upset enough as it is, going on about her blooming Tony. Jude's even stroppier than usual. Rochelle's acting extra flighty. They can't handle this the way you and I can. Just give me a few days, Dixie. Please. Don't tell on me.'

'All right then, Mum. I won't tell.'

Mum burst into tears. 'Oh darling. Thank you. Thank you so much. You promise, now?'

I found Bruce's hankie and mopped Mum's eyes. 'I promise,' I said. 'But it's just for a little bit. We'll have to tell *quite* soon. But you can pretend for now if it makes you happy.'

'You're such a good girl to me, Dixie,' Mum said, eyes brimming again. She held Sundance up and made the baby's soft cheek brush mine.

'He's giving you a kiss. He loves you so much already,' Mum whispered. 'You're his favourite big sister.'

12

Mum stayed stuck on her mattress with Sundance, as if they were marooned on a desert island. Martine and Jude and Rochelle came visiting but she sent them away, saying she was tired and wanted to rest. She didn't notice Martine had been crying. She didn't notice Jude had a sore nose. She didn't even notice Rochelle was all dressed up in her best (damp) jeans and silver sparkly top.

I was the only one Mum wanted. She let me make her a cup of tea, she let me help her to the loo, she let me fetch Sundance's clean nappies. She even let me stay while she changed her, though she kept her back to me, bending over Sundance, blocking her blatant little-girl bottom from my view.

'I'll give him a little feed now,' said Mum. 'You go off and play for a bit, Dixie. You've been such a good girl.'

I felt too grown up and important to *play*. It was so lovely to feel I was the chosen one, Mum's favourite. Sundance liked me too. I was good with babies. Maybe

I'd be a nursery nurse when I was grown up. No, I'd have my *own* nursery, and all the babies would have little white rocking cots with red and green and yellow and purple blankets so no one would know whether they were boys or girls. They'd have mobiles hanging above each cot, little birds flying round and round, and the babies would reach up with their little fat fists to try to catch them.

I'd feed them and change them and they'd all have a bath together in a special big shallow baby bath and then I'd cuddle them all in a huge white towel and tickle their tummies and play piggies with their tiny toes. I'd be Nurse Dixie and every single baby would love me and stop crying the minute I picked them up.

I thought about Mary. I wanted to stop her crying too. She didn't know how to play properly and have fun. She seemed worried about spoiling that scary baby doll. I thought about my old Barbies. They'd nearly all torn their clothes and they had skinhead haircuts and permanent gel pen tattoos. Maybe Mary could have a good game with them. It wouldn't matter in the slightest if they got spoilt.

I rummaged in my box and seized a handful of them. Rochelle was in the kitchen, trying to brush her red suede shoes.

'Got fed up playing real babies?' she said. 'Now we're back to normal and little braindead Dixie's playing dollies.'

'*I'm* not going to be playing with them,' I said haughtily. 'I thought my friend Mary might like them. I'm going to show *her* how to play.'

'Who do you think you are, Mary blooming Poppins?'

said Rochelle. 'And actually, they're not *your* Barbies, they're mine, and you haven't half ruined them! What's happened to their *hair*? Have you cut it all off?'

'You shut up, or I'll cut *your* hair off,' I said, and then I rushed out the back door quick before she could get me.

I hitched myself up on the wall, the Barbies clutched in one hand like a weird bouquet. Mary wasn't on the swing. The baby doll wasn't there in its buggy. The garden was empty.

I sat on the wall, swinging my legs. I waited. Then I got fed up with waiting. I decided it would be fun to arrange the Barbies in a little circle just inside Mary's gate, with their right arms all raised as if they were waving to her. She'd have a little laugh when she found them.

I jumped over my wall, crossed the alley, carefully opened the stiff latch and crept inside. I squatted down by the gate and propped each Barbie up against it, their hands up. They looked much dirtier in Mary's garden, their haircuts more brutal. I'd tipped all their breasts with red felt pen and now I wished I hadn't. I licked my finger and tried rubbing their chests hard to get it off.

'What are you up to, eh?'

I was so startled I fell backwards on my bottom. I looked up, scarlet in the face. A man was staring down at me. He had huge scary scissors in his hand. I gave a little squeal.

'Hey, hey, it's all right. Don't be frightened!' He saw me looking at the awful scissors and dropped them on the grass. 'It's all right, they're just my pruning shears. My little girl doesn't like them either.'

'You're Mary's dad?' I said.

'You know my Mary?'

I nodded, but I didn't say she was my friend. I didn't want to get her into trouble. But he was smiling at me now. He bent down and helped pull me up. The Barbies trembled and then fainted simultaneously.

'Are these your dollies? Why were you putting them in my garden? What are they, Pretty Maids all in a row?'

'I thought Mary might like to play with them,' I whispered.

'What a nice thought,' he said, though he looked at the Barbies a bit doubtfully.

'Can I see her?'

'Well, I think she's finishing her tea right now,' he said. 'She's a bit of a picky eater, our Mary. She's in trouble with her mum for not eating her crusts. Do you eat your crusts?'

I nodded, though I was fibbing.

He took a deep breath. 'Well, why don't you come in and show Mary a good example, eh?'

I gathered up the swooning Barbies and trotted along beside him, up the green striped lawn to the patio. He paused at their back door.

'Wipe your feet, dear. My wife's a bit particular. Very very houseproud.' He took his own gardening shoes off and walked indoors in his fluffy socks. I followed him on tiptoe.

I couldn't believe their house. Their kitchen looked like it was still in a showroom, brand new and pin-neat, every pan in place and shining like a little sun. The kitchen table was scrubbed clean and totally bare. They didn't eat in there.

151

They had a special dining room where they had their tea. It was rose-pink with dark gleaming furniture. The dining-room table had a fancy white cloth on it, its scalloped edges stiff with embroidery. It was still set for tea time, with special rosy plates and cups and saucers. There was a big plate containing a few sandwiches, another plate of chocolate biscuits and a third plate with a big iced sponge cake topped with cherries. There were a couple of slices missing, so I could see the thick jam and buttercream. My mouth started watering.

Mary was sitting up very straight, a plate of four crusts in front of her. They were in a square, like a frame without a picture. Mary's mother was standing beside her, arms folded, her mouth in a straight line. They both looked astonished to see me.

'Not you again!' said Mary's mother.

'I invited her in, love,' said Mary's dad. 'She's brought a little present for our Mary, isn't that nice of her?'

Mary's mother looked at my Barbies as if they were cockroaches. 'Yes, very nice, but Mary has her own dolls, dear,' she said. 'She doesn't want yours.'

There was a cabinet of dolls right behind her. They were dressed like old-fashioned little girls in pink and lilac and lemon smocked dresses, with flouncy petticoats and white socks and tiny black patent shoes. They all had pink cheeks and dimples and were smiling widely, showing off their little pearly teeth. Some had glossy ringlets and ribbons, some had short curls and heart-shaped hairslides, some had very neat nylon plaits.

'Are *they* Mary's dolls?' I asked, awed.

'Good heavens, no. They're *my* dolls, my Dimpled

Darlings special collection. They're collector's items,' said Mary's mother.

I couldn't help thinking she'd like to keep Mary in a cabinet too, squeaky clean and dusted, dimples permanently in place. Mary was blinking at me, nibbling her lip.

'I've come to tea!' I said, trying to reassure her.

Mary's mother frowned. 'Not today, dear. Off you run now. And take your dollies with you.'

'I asked her, love,' said Mary's dad. 'I thought it might help our Mary learn to eat up her crusts. Sit yourself down then. What's your name?'

'Dixie.'

'Wait a minute . . . Dixie,' said Mary's mum. She said my name as if it was a rude word. She thrust a glossy magazine on the pink and white striped seat of the dining chair, as if she thought my bottom would sully it. The magazine felt cold and uncomfy and it crackled whenever I moved. I fidgeted from buttock to buttock, not sure whether I should help myself to a sandwich or not. At home you just grabbed, but everything was so different in Mary's house.

Mary's mother offered me the plate, making it like a little ritual. I took two sandwiches, one in each hand, so she wouldn't have to go through the whole rigmarole again. She frowned at me, so I guessed this was a mistake. I ate the sandwiches quickly, taking alternate bites. One was cream cheese and cucumber, the other some sort of fishy stuff with green leafy bits. They weren't very nice.

'Oh, yummy,' I said politely. 'Look, Mary, I'm eating my crusts all up.'

They were quite hard crusts, with a burnt taste. I

could see how they'd stick in your throat and stop you swallowing. I chewed hard but the crusts took ages to turn into mush. My teeth were all gummed up with them. I'd simply spit them out at home but this obviously wasn't an option.

'The crusts are extra yummy, Mary,' I mumbled through my mouthful.

Mary looked at me forlornly. I felt like I was betraying her.

'Don't worry, I never ate crusts when I was your age though,' I said.

'Are you going to eat your crusts now, Mary?' said her dad.

Mary nodded, but when she tried poking a crust into her mouth I saw her shudder and retch. The crust slid out of her mouth, slippery and revolting.

'Dear, dear, Mary,' said her mother. She said it softly, but it sounded like a threat.

'Would you like a slice of cake now, Dixie?' said Mary's dad.

'Oooh yes. Please!' I said. I glanced at Mary. 'Can she have cake now too?'

'Yes, of course she can have some cake. In a minute. When she's eaten up those crusts,' said Mary's mum.

I ate a slice of cake. It was lovely, but I couldn't enjoy it. I wolfed it down to get rid of it, and choked, spraying crumbs everywhere. I felt myself going red again. 'Can I have a drink of water?' I gasped.

I didn't really need it. I thought if Mary's mum went to get it I'd have a chance to grab Mary's crusts off her plate and gobble them up for her. But Mary's dad went to get it. Mary's mum stood over Mary like a jailer.

'You'd better run along now, dear. Perhaps you'd like to take a slice of sponge for your sister?' She smiled graciously.

'Dixie's got three sisters,' Mary whispered.

Four, I thought.

Mary's mother made me up a paper napkin parcel of cake. 'Four slices,' she said.

'It's home-made,' said Mary's father proudly. 'Not many women find time to bake their own cakes nowadays.'

Mary's mother simpered and smoothed her blonde curls. She seemed so pretty and so sweet but she couldn't fool me.

I stood up to go. I swallowed hard. 'Mary's not going to get smacked for not eating her crusts, is she?' I said.

Mary's mother frowned. Her dad looked shocked.

'We don't ever smack our Mary,' he said.

'Whatever gave you that idea?' said Mary's mother.

I looked at Mary helplessly but kept my mouth shut.

Mary's dad ushered me out the dining room, back down the hall, through the spotless kitchen to the back garden.

'Mary can be a bit stubborn at times, I'm told. "Mary Mary, quite contrary," like the nursery rhyme. Oh, you forgot your dollies. I think it's best you take them home, dear.'

I ran back to the dining room where I'd dropped them. Mary and her mum were still at the table. Mary's mum was pinching Mary's nose so that her mouth fell open. She rammed the crusts right down her throat, so hard that Mary's head jerked backwards.

I gasped in terror. Mary's mum straightened up. She smiled at me.

'There!' she said. 'Mary's eaten up all her crusts like a good girl.'

Mary sat still, tears streaming down her face, her cheeks bulging with crusts. I went to run for Mary's dad. He was standing behind me.

'Well done, Mary,' he said.

I didn't know if he'd seen or not. I knew there was no point in telling.

I grabbed my Barbies and then ran back to my own house. I threw the cake under a bush in the garden. I kept shaking my head, trying to pretend it hadn't happened. I didn't know what to do.

I went running to Mum.

'Here's my little helper,' said Mum. 'Are you hungry, sweetheart? Your best pal Bruce has gone off to get us all pizzas.'

'Mum . . .'

'What?'

'Why are some mums so horrid?'

'Do what, love? You mean me?'

'No!'

'Some of those nosy interfering cows back at Bletchworth used to say I wasn't a good mum. One of them even called in the social workers when you were little, thinking I wasn't feeding you proper. Blooming cheek! I didn't half give her an earful.'

Sundance started whimpering in Mum's arms.

'What's up with you, darling? More milky? There's nothing wrong with *your* appetite, is there? You'd feed all the time, wouldn't you, my son? What a little greedy guts! Still, that's boys for you.'

I backed away from Mum. I hated her going on like that. Mums weren't *supposed* to pretend.

'Are you feeling OK, Dixie?' said Bruce, when I only

156

nibbled at the edge of the giant pizza he'd bought for tea.

'I'm fine,' I lied.

Martine wasn't hungry either. She only ate half a slice of pizza, picking out button mushrooms and slices of tomato and peppers and arranging them on her plate: two mushroom eyes, a blobby pepper nose, a grinning tomato mouth, making a weird baby face. It was the sort of game *I* usually played.

'Stop playing with your food and *eat* the flipping thing,' I said in Mum's voice.

Martine didn't laugh.

Rochelle didn't eat much either, because she was hoping Ryan would treat her at McDonald's.

'You girls are so picky,' said Bruce.

'I'm not,' said Jude. She wolfed slice after slice, scarcely swallowing.

'Well, you've been working hard,' said Bruce.

Jude grinned at him. 'Do you think I'm any good at Wing Chun?'

'You know you are. You're a natural,' said Bruce.

He thrust his clenched fist towards her chest and she immediately blocked it. They both laughed.

'You shouldn't encourage her,' said Martine. 'She'll only get in more fights, and the boys round here are really scary. They probably carry knives.'

'They're not all scary. Some are pretty cool looking,' said Rochelle.

Jude frowned at her. 'You're such a fool, Rochelle. Why are you all tarted up, eh? Where are you going?'

'Just because you like to dress like a scruff doesn't mean we all have to do the same. I felt like putting on my decent clothes, OK?'

'You look a sight. You've got half a vat of make-up smeared all over your face.'

'Take a look in the mirror if you want a *real* fright,' said Rochelle. 'I'm off.'

'You're not going out, Rochelle. Martine, stop her,' said Jude.

Martine wasn't paying attention. She was texting Tony, her finger going stab stab stab at the buttons on her phone. Jude yelled at her. Martine sighed.

'*You* stop her, Jude. I've got other stuff to think about.'

'You're the eldest.'

'I'm not going to be here much longer. Then *you'll* be the eldest. See how *you* like it.' Martine marched off upstairs, still texting.

'OK, I'm in charge now,' said Jude. 'You're not allowed out the house, Rochelle, do you hear me?'

'I hear you. I can hardly *help* hearing you, you're bellowing right in my ear,' said Rochelle. 'But I don't have to do what you say.'

'She's talking sense, Roxanne,' said Bruce. 'You can't go off by yourself. You're not old enough.'

Rochelle stood up, tossing back her golden curls. 'Number one – my name is *Rochelle*. Number two – I'm a teenager, very nearly, and can do what I please. Number three – *you* certainly can't boss me about, Mr Weirdo Guy.' She flounced out of the room.

'I'll tell Mum,' Jude called.

'And I'll tell Mum you've been fighting,' Rochelle yelled.

She slammed right out of the front door, banging it hard. There was a second of silence. Then we heard the baby start wailing.

'*Shall* we tell Mum?' I asked.

'I think so,' said Jude.

'I *know* so,' said Bruce. 'I'll tell her, and then I'd better go after Miss Fancy Pants, though she certainly won't thank me for it.'

He knocked on the living-room door and then tried to go in. Mum was starting to change Sundance. She told Bruce to go away. She used short, sharp words.

Bruce looked very put out when he came back. 'Your mum was very rude to me,' he said.

'She's not herself,' I said quickly.

'I'm only trying to help,' said Bruce. 'Roxanne – Rochelle – whatever – shouldn't be strutting round an estate like this all by herself. Look what happened to Jude, and she's older and got a lot more sense.'

Jude looked pleased at this. 'Let's go after her in your van, Bruce.'

I went with them. We drove up and down Mercury Street. Our end was the worst, with many of the houses boarded up. Some of the houses at the other end had curtains at the windows and neat grass at the front. Several even had flowers and little white picket fences.

'Maybe it's not too bad round here after all,' said Bruce.

Then he drove through the tower-block entrance. We looked up at the stained concrete and rusted railings, up and up and up, to the very top.

'I wonder if you can get out on the roof?' said Jude.

'I've just said you were a girl with common sense,' said Bruce. 'How could you have such a crazy idea?'

'I went up on the roof heaps of times in our old flats,' said Jude. 'It was my territory.'

Some boys went rattling past on skateboards, bashing on the van and making rude signs at us.

'It looks like it's their territory, Jude, like it or lump it. You try going up those stairs again and they'll likely toss you right over the balcony.'

'Wait till I get the hang of this Wing Chun,' Jude muttered. 'I'll go anywhere I want and no one will dare lift a finger.'

'Dream on, girl,' said Bruce. 'There's a limit, even with martial arts. It's fine in the movies – Bruce Lee can take on any number of opponents and *chop-chop-chop-kick* they all go flying. Their weapons hurtle up into the air and circle back and they get sliced to ribbons with their own swords. But it's fantasy, Jude. A little game of Let's Pretend.'

I was playing my own game of Let's Pretend. I played Bruce was our real uncle and he was taking us out for a drive in his van and we were going to Disneyland, a brand-new one conveniently situated down the road and round the corner. We'd hurtle up Space Mountain and whiz round the Indiana Jones ride and all the other stuff the kids at my old school showed off about. I'd maybe get a little bit scared. Uncle Bruce would sit me on his knee and tell me he'd look after me, and I didn't have to worry about anything any more. I didn't have to worry about my new friend Mary, I didn't have to worry about my mum, I didn't have to worry about any of my sisters – not even my brand-new baby sister in her blue boys' outfits.

When we were done with all the rides we'd go and have tea in McDonald's, and Uncle Bruce wouldn't nag me about eating meat; he'd buy me a portion of french fries and I'd share them chip for chip with Bluebell.

I thought of Bluebell without her head. I could see the stuffing, the sad dead body.

160

I couldn't tell.

But what if something bad really happened to Rochelle?

'I don't think Rochelle's round here,' I said. 'I have a feeling she might just be in McDonald's.'

'You have a *feeling*?' said Jude. 'Oh, Dixie, you're impossible. Why didn't you *say*?'

'You hate telltales.'

'Yeah, but that's only if you tell tales on *me*,' said Jude. 'You must always always always snitch on Rochelle because she's so stupid she'll get up to anything. So why McDonald's? Is she meeting someone there? Dixie, *tell*!'

'She said she'd tear Bluebell's head off if I did,' I said, clutching Bluebell tight in both hands. I could feel her small bird-heart beating under her feathers. She gave tiny cheeps of terror.

'I won't let her, don't worry, Dixie,' said Bruce.

'She *is* meeting someone?'

I wriggled my shoulders. 'Maybe.'

'But she doesn't know anyone here.' Then Jude clapped her hand over her mouth. 'Oh God. Not the guy with the earring, the one I beat up?'

Jude didn't beat up any of them the way I remembered it, but maybe she liked pretending too. I nodded.

'I can't believe she could be such an idiot! And you're an idiot too, Dixie, keeping quiet about it.'

'Hey, hey, that's unfair! It's not Dixie's fault,' said Bruce.

He drove out of the Mercury block, passing Neptune and Mars and Saturn and Venus and Jupiter, all as towering and terrifying. He headed towards the town.

'It's quite a walk. Rochelle was wearing her wibble-wobble heels. Maybe she won't have got there yet,' said

161

Jude. She reached over and took hold of my hand. 'Sorry, Dix. Of course it's not your fault.'

'Do you think he might hit her, like the boys hit you, Jude?'

'No,' said Jude, though she didn't sound sure.

'Might he do worse things?' I whispered.

'Stop it,' said Bruce. 'You're just frightening yourselves. He's not going to do anything untoward in McDonald's, for goodness' sake.'

'But he could take her off anywhere afterwards,' said Jude. 'Can't we go any quicker?'

'It's not going to help if I get done for speeding,' said Bruce, but he put his foot down on the accelerator.

We drove round the streets in the town centre, Jude staring at one side, me the other, straining to see the familiar golden M.

'There it is!' I cried.

Bruce parked the van on a double yellow line while Jude and I went running inside. There was no sign of Rochelle. I chewed on my fingers, panicking. Jude spotted a sign to the seating upstairs. She went rushing up and up, past the toilets and into the big room above. I went charging after her.

We saw Rochelle sitting in the corner, side by side with Ryan. Their heads were close. They were gazing into each other's eyes. Rochelle had her favourite McFlurry ice cream but her spoon was poised in mid-air. She was obviously so entranced she was forgetting all about eating. Ryan didn't look at all like he wanted to hit her or hurt her. He was gazing at her as if she was a princess with a jewelled crown on top of her long fair hair. Rochelle and Ryan seemed to shine in their own little spotlight, as if the McDonald's yellow arch was giving out its own golden glow.

I stopped still. I felt we should tiptoe away. Jude hesitated too, but then she marched over to them.

'Leave my sister alone!' she yelled, though Ryan wasn't even touching Rochelle.

'Oh God, it's not you again,' said Ryan. 'What your *problem*?'

'Take no notice of her. She's just my crazy sister,' said Rochelle. She spotted me hovering in the background. 'And there's my *other* crazy sister who's going to be very very sorry she's told on me.'

'Come home at once, Rochelle,' Jude shouted, a little too loudly. Everyone upstairs in McDonald's was starting to stare at us.

'We haven't *got* a home any more,' said Rochelle. 'I don't want to go back to that messy dump, thanks very much.'

'You're coming home *now*,' said Jude, tugging at Rochelle's arm.

'Leave her be!' said Ryan.

'Don't take any notice of her. I suppose she just can't help being jealous,' said Rochelle smugly.

'How *dare* you!' said Jude, tugging harder.

Rochelle tried to pull free. Jude hung on grimly. Rochelle's arm got a little bit twisted. She started shrieking loudly.

'Don't you dare try to push me about!' said Jude, letting go of Rochelle. She squared up to Ryan. She did her best to position herself feet apart, knock-kneed, all set to trap her goat. 'So you want a fight, do you? Come on, then!'

'I don't want to fight you. I don't fight girls. Especially not Rochelle's sisters,' said Ryan.

Rochelle fluttered her eyelashes at him adoringly. Jude was left hovering above them, at a loss.

'Just go home, Jude. I'm fine. Ryan's going to see me home. I won't be late. There's no need to get so worked up. You're just making a complete fool of yourself,' said Rochelle.

'Jude, please, let's go back to Uncle Bruce,' I begged.

'Yes, both of you bog off back to creepy Uncle Weirdo,' said Rochelle.

'He's *not* creepy Uncle Weirdo!' I shouted. 'Don't you dare call him that!'

Rochelle dared say worse things.

I flew at her, beating her chest and pulling her long golden hair. Rochelle yelled her head off.

'Oi, that's enough! Out of here!' yelled the McDonald's security guy.

He seized me in one big hand, Jude in the other, and dragged us both across the room and down the stairs.

Bruce came rushing in the entrance, looking anxious. 'What are you doing with these girls? Don't drag them like that!' he said to the McDonald's man.

'You should look after your kids properly. Sisters, are they? Fancy attacking that pretty little girl upstairs!'

'Oh Jude!' said Bruce, shaking his head at her.

'It's the little one who's the real spitfire,' said the McDonald's man. 'Going at it hell for leather!'

'*Dixie?*' said Bruce.

Then he saw a traffic warden coming along the road. 'Uh-oh! Quick, or I'll get a ticket. Are you going to let the girls go now?'

'Well, I don't know about that. I could call the cops.'

'No, wait!' It was Rochelle, running up to us. 'Look,

they're crazy, both of them, and I hate them to bits, but they're my sisters, so you won't actually arrest them, will you?'

'Oh for pity's sake – look, just go home with your dad, all of you.'

'He's not our *dad*!' said Rochelle.

'I'm jolly glad I'm not!' said Bruce. 'Come on, get in the van quick. You too, Rochelle.'

She argued bitterly, not wanting to leave Ryan.

Jude slammed into the van too, still furious. 'Fat lot of use learning Wing Chun defence when stupid guys won't try to hit you,' she muttered.

'Just as well he didn't take a swing at you. You're a natural, picking things up a treat, but you've got to train for months and months, girl, I told you that. Maybe we can find a proper club round here. Perhaps you'd better join too, Dixie! Were you *really* fighting?'

'I only fought a little bit,' I said. 'You know you said you were glad you're not our dad? Well, what about being our uncle?'

'I'll always want to be your uncle, Dixie, even if you get into more fights than Lennox Lewis,' said Bruce, chuckling. 'Just don't take a swing at me, that's all I ask.'

13

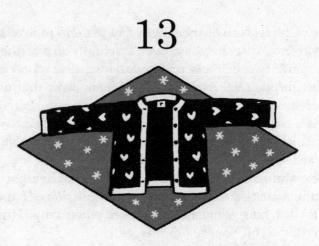

When we got back to Mercury Street I shut my eyes tight. I wished so hard I thought my head would burst. I wished that all the houses were whole and neat and newly painted with flowery gardens. I wished our house was the brightest and the best, with fairy lights hanging in the windows, roses rambling round our door, and a fountain in the front garden with a little marble mermaid spouting water into a turquoise pool.

I wished our house was beautiful inside, with satin curtains and velvet sofas and Persian rugs. I wished we'd find Mum dancing around in her slinky skirt and stilettos, all bouncy and bubbly, the way she used to be. I wished we'd find Sundance kicking his little legs on his blue changing mat, nappy off to show his little willy. I wished that my dad was there on a visit. He had a brand-new beautiful cardigan for me, a black one that wouldn't show the dirt, embroidered all over with little red hearts to prove how much he loved me. He'd put it on me and hug me and promise he was going to come and see me every single day for the rest of my life.

I wished Bluebell was real and flying freely round and round the garden. I wished Mary could come and play in our garden too, and run around roaring with laughter, her hair tumbling over her shoulders, free of those tight little plaits. I thought of that little blue vein throbbing in her forehead. I knew I should do something.

'Are you asleep, Dixie?' Bruce asked, patting me on the shoulder. 'Come on, lovey, out the van. We're home.'

'Do you believe wishes can ever come true, Uncle Bruce?'

'I'd give anything to make your wishes come true, little 'un, but I'm not magic.'

However, Bruce had worked quite a lot of magic in the house already. It smelled clean and fresh with all his lovely white lilies and roses and freesias. Mum had stuck them here and there in the living room, but she'd not given any further thought to getting it straight. She was lying back on the mattress with Sundance, furniture and cardboard boxes still crammed tightly in a ring around her.

Rochelle and Jude came crowding in, both of them complaining at the tops of their voices. Mum shut her eyes as if she was wishing too.

'*Mum!* Aren't you even listening? Jude just *totally* embarrassed me. She behaved like an idiot with Ryan, and then Dixie started *attacking* me.'

'This Ryan is years older than Rochelle. She thinks she's absolutely it because she's got a boyfriend. She doesn't have a clue. She'll end up a teenage mum if she's not careful. Tell her, Mum.'

'Shut up, Jude,' said Martine, coming into the room too. 'What have you done to your nose? Have you been fighting again? Mum, look at her!'

'Mum, should you tell on someone even if they beg you not to and say they'd get into trouble?' I asked.

'You should never ever tell. And you're in big big trouble, you and your stupid bird,' said Rochelle, snatching up my sleeve.

'Mum! She's got Bluebell!'

'I'll get her back,' Jude yelled, making a grab at Rochelle.

'Stop shouting, you two, you'll wake the baby. Here, Mum, you need to lie down properly. I'll mind the baby for you,' said Martine.

'No!' Mum opened her eyes, blinking in the sudden brightness. 'You leave him be. He's fine with me. Look, will you all please push off. You're doing my head in, all of you. I just want to be left in peace.'

'Don't worry, Sue, I'll get them sorted,' said Bruce.

'*I'll* sort them. I'm the oldest,' said Martine. 'I don't know what's up with you, Mum. You went on and on at me to come to this dump because you said you couldn't manage without me and yet now you won't let me do a blessed thing for the baby.'

'You can get some of this furniture shifted and try to make the place halfway decent. I can't stand lying with all this rubbish all around me,' said Mum.

'I'm not lifting all that stuff. It's much too heavy. I'll hurt myself,' said Martine.

'Ooh, precious,' Jude mocked. '*I'll* move it, Mum.'

'Who do you think you are, Jude? Ms Supergirl? You think you're it, don't you, charging round everywhere,

168

throwing your weight about. You might have been looked up to back at Bletchworth but everyone just laughs at you here,' said Rochelle.

'Shut up, Rochelle,' I said, grabbing Bluebell back. 'Take no notice, Jude. I'll help with the furniture.'

'You're not shifting anything, Dixie, you're far too small. You'll be the one who'll hurt herself,' Bruce said from the doorway. 'Come on, girls, stop plaguing your mum. She's still not well. Maybe we can try a bit of teamwork and get the furniture shifted all together.'

'Can I be on your team, Uncle Bruce?' I begged.

'I'm going to be the boss, little 'un, getting you all organized. It's about time too. You girls all need taking in hand.'

'Excuse me?' said Mum. 'You're the boss of *my* daughters? They need taking in hand, do they? And whose hand would that be, eh? *Yours?* What a badword cheek!' She struggled up off the mattress and went striding over to him, hands on her hips, her big bosoms bouncing.

'Now look, Sue, I didn't mean anything,' Bruce said nervously. 'It was just a figure of speech. I just meant we needed to sort it out, moving the furniture, seeing as I daren't do anything daft with my back.'

'You and your bogging back,' said Mum. 'I reckon you just say that as an excuse because you're bone idle, like all men. You're fit enough to play silly beggars with my girls, teaching them this daft kung fu fiddlesticks. As if they need any encouragement fighting! You want to teach our Jude how *not* to fight, you daft pillock.'

Bruce rocked backwards on his feet, blinking behind his glasses.

'Don't get upset, Uncle Bruce. Mum doesn't really mean it, she's just in a strop,' I said, taking his hand.

'I am not in a strop, you lippy little madam!' Mum shouted. 'Stop snuggling up to him, Dixie. He's not your uncle, he's practically a stranger.'

Bruce let go my hand. 'I *was* a stranger – and I'd have been very happy to keep it that way too. I was just helping out with the van at first, that was the deal. For a bit of spare cash, although the only cash that's been spent so far has been my own. But I kind of got sucked into all this kerfuffle and so I tried to do the decent thing and help you and your girls. *I* didn't start the uncle thing, it was all little Dixie's idea. I was tickled pink as she's a great little kid. Still, I can see it's upsetting you, so we'll stop it now. Blow my bad back, I'll do my best to get your furniture upstairs and then I'll be off. For good.'

'No!' I wailed, clinging to him.

'Stop that nonsense, Dixie, you're showing me up,' Mum snapped. 'You're just being silly now.'

I looked Mum straight in the eyes. 'You're being silly too, Mum,' I said. I looked over at little Sundance abandoned on the mattress.

Mum looked too. She suddenly shut up. 'My baby,' she whispered, and went back to the mattress. She cradled Sundance, kissing the tufty hair.

Martine and Jude and Rochelle shook their heads in disbelief. Mum was usually incapable of shutting up when she went off on one of her rants. She always yelled herself hoarse and then she'd burst into noisy tears and give us all a hug and say she was a bad-tempered old bag and the worst mum in the world and we'd all be better off in care. Then we'd hug her back and tell her she was the *best* mum in the world and we didn't want to live with anyone else but her even if she *was* a bad-tempered old bag.

'Please please please don't go, Uncle Bruce,' I said.

'I *have* to go back home, Dixie. I've got to be up at crack of dawn to get to the flower market. But don't worry, dear, I'll keep in touch, if it's OK with your mum.'

'And you'll still be my uncle?' I asked.

Bruce glanced at Mum. She was rocking the baby, not bothering with either of us any more.

'If you want,' he whispered.

'I don't want you to be my soppy old uncle, but I need you to be my Wing Chun instructor,' said Jude.

'You're on,' said Bruce. 'Come on then, let's get some of this blessed furniture upstairs. It looks like it's just you and me doing the heaving and hauling.'

'I *would* help, but I can't,' said Martine. Her hands were cupped over her tummy.

'You got a stomach ache then?' said Jude.

'Yeah,' Martine said quickly.

'Yeah, me too,' said Rochelle.

'Rubbish!' I said.

'Fat lot you know about it, Dixie,' said Rochelle.

'Well OK, I'll help,' I said. 'I can, I can, I'm much stronger than I look, Uncle Bruce.' I took off my cardie and flexed my arms to show him.

'You've got muscles like little peanuts, sweetheart,' said Bruce. He rolled his own sleeves up in a businesslike fashion. He couldn't help flexing his own muscles proudly. It looked like he had an orange inside each skinny arm.

'Wow, Mr Body Builder!' said Jude. 'That's not from Wing Chun, is it?'

'I did use to go down the gym a lot too,' said Bruce.

'Get you, Freda Flowershop,' said Rochelle. 'Hey, Martine, can I borrow your mobile a sec? I want to text someone.'

'Not that creep in McDonald's!' said Jude.

'No, you can't have my mobile, *I* need it,' said Martine. 'What creep?'

'Get out of the way, all of you,' said Jude. 'Why *can't* you help, Martine? I know it's not your time of the month, so don't use that as an excuse.'

'Will you just shut up, Jude! I've got a stomach bug, if you must know. I feel sick.'

'Rubbish!' said Jude.

'It's not rubbish, Jude, I heard her being sick this morning,' I said. I was trying to be helpful but Martine looked horrified.

'Shut *up*, Dixie. Can't you ever keep your mouth shut?' she hissed.

'Yeah, she's the biggest telltale-tit ever,' said Rochelle.

'I *can* keep secrets! I can keep the most *amazing* secrets, so you two just shut up yourselves. Just you wait till you find out *my* secret!'

'Dixie!' Mum was shouting from the living room. 'Come in here! I need you. *Now!*'

'I'll help you, Mum,' said Martine, pushing me out the way.

'No, Martine, I want Dixie.'

'Oh, all right, then, suit yourself,' said Martine huffily, flouncing off.

'*Please* lend us your mobile, Martine,' said Rochelle,

running after her. 'Hey, Jude, do my stuff first, eh? I want to get my room sorted. But be careful, don't bash it all about. Watch my dressing table, won't you?'

'You watch it or we'll bash you all about, Roxanne,' said Bruce. 'Don't go giving us your orders. We're not the removal men. We're doing this as a favour, aren't we, Jude?'

'Spot on, Bruce,' said Jude.

She dragged Rochelle's bed out of Mum's room, tipping it on its side. She looked as if she'd like to tip Rochelle right over too.

'Dixie!' Mum said urgently. 'Come in here. Come nearer!'

I squatted beside her on the mattress.

'Now look, stop hinting stuff! Your sisters aren't idiots even though they act like it most of the time. You and me have a pact, kiddo. You swore you wouldn't breathe a word.'

'Only for a few days, Mum.'

'A few weeks?'

'That's not going to work, Mum. Imagine pushing Sundance down the shops in a buggy and people stopping you and doing all that coo-coo ga-ga Is-it-a-boy-or-a-girl? stuff. You can't say he's a little boy and then a few weeks later start putting her in a little pink dress.'

'I won't speak to anyone. They're a load of nutters and no-hopers round here anyway.' Mum paused. 'Maybe that's me. Ms Nutter No-Hope, who can't provide for her kids or find one single decent guy to be their dad. I knew we couldn't stay in Bletchworth for all sorts of reasons but why did I ever think this dump

173

was the answer? I've just landed us in a worse mess. I got it all wrong – all the charts, the cards, the crystal ball. I got my baby wrong wrong wrong. I so wanted a boy, Dixie. I need my little baby boy. Don't take him away from me, please, darling. Let me keep him for a bit longer.'

Mum started crying. Sundance started wailing too, threshing sadly in her blue blanket. She smelled as if her nappy needed changing, but Jude and Bruce would be in and out all the time, shifting the furniture upstairs.

'Let me take Sundance upstairs to the bathroom and I'll change her— *him*,' I said. 'Don't cry, Mum. I won't breathe another word about our secret, I promise. Sundance can stay a boy for a bit if it'll really make you happy.'

I picked Sundance up and carried her carefully out of the room. Jude and Bruce were halfway up the stairs with Rochelle's bed. Bruce was sweating, his glasses misting up.

'You be careful, Uncle Bruce,' I said anxiously.

'I'll be OK – if I take it – slowly,' he panted.

Jude hauled, Bruce pushed, and they got the bed to the top of the stairs.

'I want it under the window,' said Rochelle. 'No, hang on, maybe it would be better against the wall.'

'*You* shove it wherever you want it, Lady Muck,' said Jude. 'Come on, Bruce, mate. Are you all right?'

'Sure,' said Bruce, though he was leaning against the wall, trying to catch his breath.

'Leave Rochelle's stuff. You go and have a sit down, Uncle Bruce. You look done in,' I said.

174

He just chuckled at me and walked stiffly downstairs.

I took Sundance into the bathroom and gingerly unpeeled her. She wasn't just wet. It was far worse than I'd imagined. I didn't know what to do.

'Please hurry up and get toilet trained,' I said to my little sister, rolling my cardie sleeves right up.

I tore off a wad of loo roll, seized her by the ankles and started dabbing at her. I dabbed and dabbed and dabbed. I wondered if it would be better to give her a bath. I didn't know *how* you bathed a baby. She was so little. I was scared I might drop her if she was all slippery with soap. Her head was too wobbly and she wriggled too much.

I managed the best I could, and then squidged the dirty nappy into a plastic carrier bag.

'There now, little Sundance. All clean and dry. Try to stay that way, eh? You're a lovely little baby but I wish you didn't have a bottom.'

It would be so easy if Sundance was like a little doll with smooth plastic instead of rude bits. Then she'd never need to be changed and no one would ever find out she was a little girl. Mum could play she was her special boy and no one would know any different. If no one had bottoms we could choose which sex we wanted to be all the time we were growing up. I could have been a boy, then I could always be Mum's favourite. Jude would be a boy too, even though she didn't seem to like them. Rochelle *loved* boys but I couldn't imagine her as anything else but the girliest girl. Martine was very girly too, even when she dressed up in Tony's big T-shirts or his black leather jacket.

I heard Jude and Bruce struggling back up the stairs.

I picked Sundance up and took her to watch from the landing. They were hauling Rochelle's unwieldy dressing table, both of them cursing as the drawers rattled and slid about.

'We should have taken the drawers out first,' Bruce gasped. 'I'm not thinking straight. Here, if we prop it against the wall can you balance it for a moment? Then I can edge up beside you and deal with the drawers.'

'What's she got *in* here? Something stinks!' said Jude.

As if in answer, the bottom drawer shot out. Sundance's first dirty nappy flew threw the air. It landed on poor Bruce's head.

He dodged sideways, shaking his head, still trying to hang onto the dressing table. Then he yelled. It was a horrible, high-pitched scream.

'Uncle Bruce!' I went hurtling down the stairs, clutching Sundance to my chest.

'Here, Bruce, I've got the poxy dressing table safe,' said Jude, heaving it away from him.

Bruce crouched on the stairs, back bent over.

'Uncle Bruce, are you all right?' I called.

'You can straighten up now, Bruce,' said Jude.

Bruce wasn't all right. He couldn't straighten up.

'I've done my back in,' he groaned.

'Was that my dressing table? Watch it, Jude, don't budge it against the wall like that, it'll get scratched,' Rochelle shouted.

She shut up when she got to the stairs and saw Bruce.

'Did someone fall?' Martine called, coming to check.

'Oh my God! Sundance? Dixie, have you dropped him?' Mum yelled. She came rushing out into the hall, her long black hair flying. Her big bosoms were nearly flopping right out of her nightie as she ran.

'Sundance is fine, Mum. I've got him. It's Uncle Bruce. He's hurt himself – and it's all my fault!' I said, starting to cry.

'Not – your fault – Dixie,' Bruce mumbled, still bent double.

'It was, it was! I stuffed the nappy in Rochelle's dressing table.'

'You did *what*?' said Rochelle. 'How *could* you, Dixie! How totally disgustingly mean of you!'

'Shut up, Rochelle, and help me get your bogging dressing table upstairs before I drop it,' said Jude.

'Are you all right, Bruce, mate?' said Mum. 'Maybe you'd better take it easy now.'

Bruce tried to shake his head totally free of the horrible nappy. He screamed again. 'Don't think – I've got – much choice,' he gasped. 'Can't move!'

'What? Of course you can move,' said Mum. 'Here, we'll get you up again. Martine, squeeze past Jude and Rochelle and help haul him up.'

'I can't *haul*,' said Martine.

'I will, I will! Take my hand, Uncle Bruce.' I flipped the last bit of nappy from his hair and held both his hands. 'Try now.'

'OK, little 'un. Give me a second – to get my breath. Then we'll see – if you can get – silly old uncle – back on his feet.'

I waited. We all waited. Bruce strained until the sweat stood out on his forehead but he couldn't stand up. He could barely move.

Jude and Martine sat on the steps above him. Mum

and I paced below him in the hall. Rochelle clattered about upstairs, dragging her furniture around in her room.

'Can't you come and help me, Jude? I've decided to have my bed over here.'

'Bog off, Rochelle. If you'd only lent a hand getting your stuff upstairs poor Bruce wouldn't be crippled up right this minute,' said Jude.

'Don't say crippled, it sounds too bloody permanent,' Mum said. She walked over to Bruce. 'What are we going to do with you, mate? Are you going to stay stuck here on the stairs for ever like a blooming carpet?'

'It's not − by choice,' Bruce mumbled.

'Come on then, stir yourself,' said Mum. 'Help me pull him, girls.'

'Don't, Mum, you'll hurt him.'

'Dixie, he can't stay here for ever. Right, Bruce, get a grip.'

We shoved, Bruce screamed. We hauled, Bruce hollered. We couldn't get him upright, but we did get him halfway there, his bottom in the air. Very very slowly, he managed to clamber down like a toddler. When he got to the hallway at long last he stayed in a crouch.

'Straighten up,' said Mum.

'I would if I could. I can't!' said Bruce.

'Oh Gawd, what are we going to do with you *now*?' said Mum.

'Should we get a doctor?' I said.

'We don't want any doctors snooping round here,' Mum said quickly. 'Anyway, we haven't *got* a doctor. I doubt anyone decent would dare come out to the Planet Estate. All the druggies would be after them.'

'I don't – need doctor,' said Bruce, teeth gritted. 'They can't – do anything. Just need – to rest – flat on back – till it's better.'

'How, long will that take then?' said Mum. 'A couple of hours?'

'A couple – of days – sometimes longer,' Bruce gasped.

'Oh! Well, looks like we've got an overnight guest, girls,' said Mum.

'No! No, I can't! Got to get home – sort the shop. If I can – make it to my van.'

Bruce tried his best but he couldn't even hobble as far as the front door. He jarred his back so badly that tears started trickling down his cheeks.

'Oh, *poor* Uncle Bruce. Look, you need to lie down *now*,' I said, steering him into the living room.

'Not in there, Dixie! That's my room now,' said Mum.

'It's the *only* room,' said Jude. 'He'll *have* to go in there, Mum.'

We pulled and prodded him in and out the furniture and then very gently pushed him down onto the big mattress.

'No! No, that's *my* mattress!' Mum protested. 'You can't settle down there! Get off it, Bruce.'

But Bruce was on it now, lying flat on his back like a dead man, trying not to move a muscle.

'Oh, thanks very much, mate!' said Mum.

'I did warn you – about my back,' Bruce whispered.

'OK, OK. I'm sorry,' said Mum. 'Well, as you've commandeered my mattress I suppose my boy and I will have to relocate upstairs.'

Mum summoned Jude and Martine and Rochelle and told them to take her stuff up to the bedroom.

'Look, Mum, I've done my fair share of lifting. *My* back hurts too,' said Jude.

'I told you, Mum, I can't lift things, I truly can't,' said Martine.

'I'm going out anyway,' said Rochelle.

'Oh no you're not,' said Mum. 'Well, thanks a bunch, girls. You're a dead helpful lot. Well, to hell with you. I need a bed if Bruce here is going to be stuck on mine. Rochelle's is upstairs already so I'll take that.'

'You can't, Mum! Where will *I* sleep?'

'You'll have to share with Martine.'

'That's not fair, Mum. I can't squash up with her. Let Dixie share, she's the littlest. Look, please please please let me go out, just for a bit. I want to see Ryan and explain that my sisters are idiots.'

'You're the idiot, having anything to do with that creep,' said Jude.

There was a big argument between Mum and Rochelle and Jude and Martine. I went and sat next to Bruce on the mattress, Sundance in my arms. Bruce had his eyes shut.

'Have you gone to sleep, Uncle Bruce?' I whispered.

'Chance would be a fine thing, with my back giving me merry hell and all that argy-bargy going on in the hall. Do they go on like this all the time, Dixie?'

'Yep.'

'It's driving me bonkers. Doesn't it get on your nerves?'

'I pretend stuff, like I have my own planet and Bluebell and I live there all by ourselves. You can come visiting on Planet Dixie if you like.'

'That's very nice of you,' said Bruce. He tried to look up at me and whimpered in pain.

Sundance was whimpering too, her little feet tangled up in her shawl.

'Here, darling, let's set you free,' I said, unwrapping her. I tickled her tummy and she waved her arms and legs around in her little blue sleeping suit. 'Hey, look, Sundance can whiz off to Planet Dixie too – she's already wearing a little baby spacesuit.'

'She?' said Bruce.

'I mean he,' I said, blushing.

'I'm like a blooming great baby now,' said Bruce, sighing.

I did wonder what on earth he was going to do about going to the loo. I thought hard about milk bottles and vases, though I knew Bruce would find this horribly embarrassing.

He solved the problem by rolling off the mattress and creeping, doubled over, to the downstairs toilet. He couldn't manage to straighten up at all, and he couldn't bear to sit either. He had to eat lying flat on his back, taking very tiny mouthfuls so he wouldn't choke. I tucked tissues all round his neck and found him a straw when he tried to drink his tea.

'You're a grand little nurse, Dixie,' said Bruce.

'Yeah, I'm good at it, aren't I!' I said, pleased with myself.

I was still number one nursemaid to Sundance. Mum got settled into Rochelle's bed upstairs but Sundance didn't seem to like the change of scenery and yelled.

'I'll see if I can calm him down,' I said grandly, going upstairs. 'Shall I take him, Mum?'

'Yes, love, walk him round for a bit, see if he'll nod off then.'

Jude and Rochelle and Martine were all watching.

'It's not fair, Mum – why do you keep choosing *Dixie*?' said Rochelle. 'He's my brother too. I want a go at holding him.'

'You're not taking one step with Sundance, not in those silly heels,' said Mum.

'*I'll* hold him for a bit,' said Jude, surprisingly. 'Look, I've got trainers on, so I'm not going to trip.'

'No way, Jude,' said Mum. 'You were always a shocker with your toys. You tugged your teddy's ears off and scalped your poor Barbie.'

'It was *my* Barbie,' said Rochelle.

'Whatever. We'll let the baby get a bit bigger before you tote him around. I want him to stay all in one piece.'

'Look, *I'm* the one who's only here because I'm supposed to be looking after the blooming baby,' said Martine bitterly.

'I need you to look after *me*, darling,' said Mum. 'How about making me another cup of tea, eh? And you'd better get the other beds upstairs somehow. Or at least the mattresses. You girls can't sleep downstairs with old Brucie Bad Back.' She sighed. 'Pity he's turned out such a liability.'

'That's not fair, Mum,' I said, walking Sundance up and down. She was settling already, her little warm head lolling in the crook of my neck. I patted her proudly. 'You *knew* Uncle Bruce had a bad back and yet you still made him shift the stuff.'

'Oh put another record on, Dixie. OK, maybe I'm not being fair to him. Who says we've got to be fair? *Life* isn't fair.' She sighed, then slipped right down under the duvet, pulling it over her head.

'But Mum—'

'Mum!'

'Mum?'

'*Mum!*'

'Will you all just go *away*. I'm sick of the lot of you. I just want to be left in peace. So push off!'

14

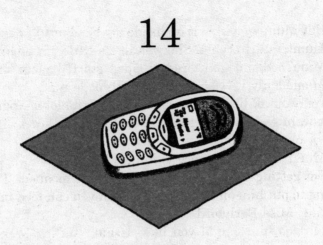

I ended up having to share a bed with Jude. It was fun at first, but I kept cuddling up too close and Jude pushed me away.

'You're like one of those little toy monkeys, Dixie. It's like you've got sticker pads on your palms and you just want to cling. I feel like I'm suffocating.'

'Bluebell will peck you if you're mean to me,' I said.

'Then I'll throw her out the bed,' said Jude, turning over and taking most of the duvet with her.

It was just as well I'm a clingy girl. I had to cling on grimly to the edge of the bed or I'd have tipped off onto the floor.

I woke up when dawn was breaking. I hate the dark because you can't see what might be creeping up on you, but it's magical when everything starts to turn silvery, as if it's been sprinkled with fairy dust. You couldn't see the bare walls and the ugly floorboards properly. Our rickety bed and the cardboard boxes could be mistaken for ornate painted chests and the finest fairytale four-poster.

I lay quietly making it up inside my head until I heard Sundance start crying. She was like a little car engine. She coughed and spluttered, stopped, started again, and then suddenly revved up into full-throttle roar.

I slid out of bed and went to find her. She was lying beside Mum, wailing away. Mum groaned, burrowing down under the duvet.

'Mum? Mum, Sundance is hungry.'

'I'm getting too old for this lark,' Mum moaned. 'I'm going to put him on a bottle soon, then you can feed him for me, Miss Earlybird.'

'I'll feed him now if you like,' I said, stuffing Mum's pillow up my nightie to make a really big chest.

'Oh Dixie, what are you like?' said Mum, grabbing the pillow back and putting it behind her head. 'Here, give me little guzzleguts.'

She took Sundance in her arms and started feeding her. I giggled at the slurping sound in the quiet house.

'She *is* a guzzleguts, isn't she, Mum?'

'*He*,' said Mum. 'Your little brother Sundance.'

'But Mum—'

'Not now, Dixie. Don't make me go all tense or we'll give Sundance hiccups. You go downstairs and make me a cup of tea, eh?'

I crept down the bare stairs, imagining rich red carpet and gilt banisters. I breathed in deeply downstairs. Bruce's lilies made everywhere smell like a beautiful garden. I felt my head and found my freesia still tangled up in my hair. I imagined Bruce coming every day and giving us all garlands of roses and carnation crowns and us stringing lilies across each room like great white paperchains.

I went to the living-room door and knocked politely. 'Uncle Bruce? Uncle Bruce, are you in there?' I whispered.

'I'm in here all right, Dixie,' he mumbled. 'Looks like I'm stuck here for the foreseeable future. My back's giving me bloody hell.'

'That's so great! I mean, I'm sorry your back's hurting, but I'm so glad you can stay. Would you like a cup of tea?'

'Yes please, little angel.'

I made two cups. I crept into the living room with Bruce's. He didn't have his glasses on. He looked a bit lost without them so I found them next to the mattress and gently edged them back onto his head. He gave his little nose a twitch and they settled into place.

He grunted whenever he lifted his head for a sip of tea. When he'd finished half the cup he lay right back and sighed deeply.

'Is it very painful, Uncle Bruce?'

'I'll live,' he said. 'Just about. Now, you'd better leave me be for a bit because I shall have to go to the toilet soon and I haven't got any trousers on. Oh Gawd, what am I going to do, stuck without pyjamas and toothbrush and shaving kit and underpants—'

'You've managed without pyjamas, you can borrow my toothbrush, Mum and Martine have both got razors – but I don't think we can help you with underpants!'

I went upstairs to give Mum her tea. She'd finished feeding Sundance and changed her too. We'd got a system going with plastic bags for used nappies now.

'I suppose I'd better get myself washed up now,' said Mum, yawning. 'I'll grab the bathroom first before all you girls go barging in and use up all the hot water.'

But before she could swing her legs out of bed someone stumbled across the landing and into the bathroom. We heard her being sick, though she was running the bath taps to mask the noise.

'Oh God,' said Mum. 'That's Martine.'

'She's got this stomach bug thing, remember? She was sick yesterday too.'

'I think I know why she's being sick. It's got damn all to do with stomach bugs!' said Mum.

'Are you cross, Mum?'

'Yes, I'm blooming mad at her, Dixie. I told her and told her to be careful. Why wouldn't she *listen*?' Mum thumped her pillow. Sundance wailed, startled.

'You quieten him, Dixie. I've got a few words to say to Martine.' Mum went storming into the bathroom.

I head Martine gasp as the door banged. Mum started shouting. Martine shouted back. It sounded like the start of an all-out Diamond big barney. Jude and Rochelle groaned sleepily.

'Dixie? Are you all right?' Bruce called from downstairs. 'What's all the shouting?'

I went down. He was crouched in the hall, duvet wrapped round him for modesty so he looked like a giant caterpillar.

'What's going on?' he groaned.

'Mum's mad at Martine.' I paused. I wasn't *that* thick. 'I think she's going to have a baby.'

Bruce blinked. 'But she's only just this minute had one!'

'Not *Mum*! Martine.'

'She's just a kid!' Bruce looked truly shocked. 'She's still at school! What a terrible waste. Fancy mucking up her life before she's even got started.'

'I'm not mucking up my life!' Martine shouted, banging out the bathroom. She stood at the top of the stairs, thin and shivering in her skimpy nightie, her hair sticking up all over the place. She didn't look like my bossy big sister Martine without her fancy hairdo and her make-up and her tight jeans and pointy boots. She looked younger than Jude, younger than Rochelle, almost as young as me.

'How dare you say I'm mucking up my life! You don't know anything about Tony and me. We're in love. I bet you've never been in love in your whole life. You're such a sad-looking old git no one would ever want you anyway. You're pathetic. You've got so little going for you in your own life you latch onto us like a leech, sucking up to my stupid little sister.'

'You shut up, Martine Diamond, or I'll smack you right in the gob!' I yelled, charging up the stairs. 'It was *me* latched onto Uncle Bruce. And *I'm* not stupid. You're the stupid one, getting pregnant.'

'Martine's going to have a *baby*?' said Rochelle, rushing out onto the landing.

'Oh, this is great! That's you and your big mouth, Mum. Now the whole family knows my business!' Martine said furiously.

'It's *my* business now,' said Mum. 'I'm the poor Joe Soap who's going to have to look after you *and* your baby, even though it's hard enough managing my own kids.'

'That's a big laugh,' said Martine. 'You can't manage yourself, let alone us. Look at us, stuck in this hideous house on the worst estate in England. The girls are running wild. Jude's getting into fights, Rochelle's going round with hoodies, Dixie's filthy dirty and running about barefoot. Oh yeah, well done, Mum. You really know how to bring up a family.'

'Give it a rest, Martine,' said Jude, coming to join us. She went to Mum and put her arm round her. 'Take no notice. She doesn't mean it, she's just upset.'

'I mean every word of it. It's true, and we all know it,' said Martine. 'How dare you lecture me, Mum. Look at you and all the guys in your life. Oh, pardon me – all the guys *no longer* in your life, like all our dads.'

'Shut your mouth, Martine,' said Jude.

'How can she see *my* dad when he's dead?' said Rochelle.

'She still sees *my* dad. Sometimes,' I said.

'What about the baby's dad? You can't fool me with that artist fairy tale. What was he, a one-night stand? I bet you don't even know his name! No wonder everyone calls you a slag back at Bletchworth,' said Martine.

We all gasped. It was the word we never said, not even to each other. We all looked at Mum. We expected her to fly at Martine. But she just stood there, looking stunned. Tears started falling down her cheeks.

Martine put her hand over her mouth, as if she wished she hadn't said it. She looked like she was starting to cry too. If only they'd been left alone they'd have both sobbed and then said sorry and they'd have a big hug and the barney would be over.

Bruce didn't understand. 'Don't you dare call your mother a slag, Martine!' he called from the bottom of the stairs. 'That's a terrible thing to say. Look, you've made her cry. Aren't you sorry?'

'No, I'm not bogging sorry!' Martine shouted. 'She *is* a slag. And she's made me cry heaps and heaps, but she's never said sorry to *me*. Well, I'm out of here now.'

'Don't go, Martine,' said Mum. 'We'll work things out. I'll look after you.'

'I don't *need* looking after. I'm going back to Bletchworth to live with Tony and his folks. I should have stayed there, like I planned. You made such a fuss about needing me to help with the baby but you won't even let me near him. You're bonkers enough to let daft little Dixie carry him round and change him but you won't let me. Every time I come near you tell me to clear off. So that's exactly what I'm going to do.' She went off to get dressed, and then started rushing round grabbing all her things and stuffing them into carrier bags.

'Mum!' I grabbed hold of her shoulder. Her old kimono split a little at the seam, but she didn't seem to notice. 'Mum, tell Martine about Sundance. Then she'll understand and she'll stay.'

Mum shook her head. She took Sundance in her arms and looked at her helplessly. 'My little boy,' she whispered.

'She's *not*!'

'Did they really all call me a slag back at Bletchworth?' Mum said.

'No! No, of course not. Martine was just being horrible. Don't take any notice of her, Mum. *I* don't care that she called me daft. Maybe we don't *care* that she's going.'

'She's not *really* going, she's just showing off,' said Mum. 'How could she get all the way back to Bletchworth by herself?'

There was a sudden bang down in the hall, like the front door slamming.

190

'She can't have gone yet! She hasn't got all her stuff. She didn't even say goodbye!' I said.

'She's just trying to scare us. She'll be back in ten minutes,' said Mum.

We waited.

Martine didn't come back.

'I'm going to go looking for her, Mum,' said Jude, stepping into her jeans and shoving on her trainers.

She was gone nearly an hour. She came back on her own.

'I've looked everywhere,' Jude said, almost in tears. 'She could have caught a bus, she could have gone anywhere – I didn't know where to look first. Then I thought about a railway station and I couldn't find it for ages; it's way over the other side of the town. She wasn't there though. I asked if they'd seen her, I asked heaps of people, describing her, but everyone just shrugged. I truly tried, Mum.'

'I know, Jude. Don't fret, darling. Maybe she's just gone round the shops, calming herself down. She'll be back soon, you'll see.'

Mum kept trying to phone Martine's mobile, but it was switched off. Mum left messages. Jude and Rochelle and I left messages. I decided to send a special secret text to Martine telling her why I was the only one Mum let care for Sundance. I was so slow at texting that I'd only got as far as 'I didn't want to tell tales but' when Mum said she wanted to try phoning again so I had to get the text cleared sharpish before she saw it.

We forgot to have breakfast. Bruce lay patiently on the mattress in the living room, but when I went to visit him I could hear his stomach rumbling. He made his own phone call to the lady who worked in his shop. She was called Iris, which seemed a perfect name for a lady who worked with flowers. I didn't like the sound of her all the same.

'Is she pretty, Uncle Bruce?'

'Mmm, I don't know. I suppose so. Though she's no spring chicken.'

'So she's more like a tough old bird?' I said hopefully.

'No, no, she's very genteel.'

'What does that mean? Posh?'

'She's got nice manners. Very ladylike. She's very kind too – she didn't make a fuss when she had to stay late on Saturday and she's going to open the shop for me today. She's being very helpful, my Iris.'

'Is she yours? You said you didn't have a girlfriend!'

'She's not my girlfriend, sweetheart,' said Bruce. 'She wouldn't look twice at a man like me!' He chuckled at the idea and then winced in pain. 'I think I'm going to have to ask Jude to go out to a chemist. Do they let kids buy painkillers? And we're all going to need a spot of lunch – and tea, come to that. Do you think your mum's up to cooking yet?'

'Mum doesn't really cook much. We play parties sometimes and she fixes us little sandwiches and cream buns and ice cream but mostly we just go down the chippy.'

'Then I suppose that's what we'll have to do today. When I can stand up properly I can maybe fix us something.'

'Can you cook then, Uncle Bruce?'

'Nothing too fancy, like, just good plain roasts and curries. I do a very tasty macaroni cheese – your mum might like that.'

'You're a very good catch, Uncle Bruce. Iris is mad not to look at you twice. So, you've never been married?'

'Nope. I don't think I'm the marrying kind, Dixie.'

'Do you think Martine will marry Tony?'

'Maybe,' Bruce said, but he sounded doubtful.

'I'd really love to be a bridesmaid in one of those long sticky-out frocks – pink or peach or lilac. No, *blue*, and then I could carry Bluebell and she'd match. I could have a proper bridesmaid's posy and she could carry a weeny raffia basket of flowers in her beak.'

'Very fetching,' said Bruce.

'Martine will be safe, won't she?'

'Of course she will,' said Bruce.

I knew he couldn't really know but I needed him to tell me even so. Mum had stopped reassuring me. She was starting to panic, phoning and phoning, while she paced around the house in her nightie and kimono.

'Shall we sort out the furniture now you're up, Mum?' said Jude. 'We could get all the boxes unpacked too.'

Mum shook her head distractedly. 'I don't want to make a home here. I hate it. We all hate it. And it's all my fault,' she said, tears brimming. 'It's a filthy dump.'

'It might be a dump but it's not filthy any more,' Bruce muttered. 'I cleaned it up, didn't I?'

'Look at all this scribbling on the walls,' Mum said despairingly.

'A quick coat of paint would soon sort it out,' said Bruce. 'You could get on to the council again. Or if you get no joy you could buy a few cans of paint and get the girls to help you. *I'd* do it if my back was up to it. A spot of white would brighten it up no end.'

'It would still be a dump if you painted it sky-blue pink,'

Mum said. 'If only I'd stayed put. It seemed so clear in the charts. I could see great changes, new opportunities; exciting challenges – but I got it all wrong. I should have stayed in Bletchworth. Even though they all called me a slag. Well. Maybe they're right.'

'You're not a slag, Mum,' said Rochelle.

'Definitely not,' said Jude. 'I'll punch anyone who says you are.'

'Of course you're not,' I said. I paused. 'What exactly *is* a slag?'

'Oh Dixie, you kill me, you really do,' said Mum, shaking her head. 'You girls are just trying to be sweet to me. I don't know why. I'm a terrible mum.'

'*I* don't want to be sweet to you,' said Bruce. 'I'm pretty damn annoyed with you, seeing as I've worked my bottom off for you and your girls and you've barely said thank you. Here I am, stuck on my back like a stag beetle, barely able to move, knowing I've got a flower shop without any flowers when the business is rapidly going down the pan as it is. But I'll tell you one thing. You're not *my* definition of a slag. A slag is a rude, rough woman, Dixie, who's got a bad mouth and rushes round drinking and chatting up all the men, and doesn't give a stuff about her children. Well, I've heard you sounding off, Sue, so I know you swear, and maybe you like a drink and going out clubbing. You've had quite a few boyfriends in your time. Maybe you don't always act like a little lady – though how should I know? But I do know one thing. Slags don't make good mums and you're a lovely mum to your kids.'

Mum blinked at Bruce, looking astonished. Then she pulled her kimono straight and tucked her hair behind her ears. 'Thank you,' she said. 'Thank you for saying that, Bruce. And thank you for all you've done for us. We couldn't have managed without you.'

I wanted this to be like a movie. I wanted Mum and Bruce to look at each other and realize their love. Then they'd fall into each other's arms. Well, Bruce would have to stay put with his bad back but Mum could fall down on top of him. They'd have a long romantic film-star kiss while music played and us girls sang and Bluebell flew over their heads like a little lovebird.

Mum went off to change Sundance, wiping her runny nose with the back of her hand. Bruce shifted uncomfortably on the mattress, groaning and grunting. They weren't really *acting* like movie stars just yet. Maybe I had to give them time.

Jude went out to get aspirins and fish and chips. I went with her because I was scared she might get into a fight. Rochelle came too, on the lookout for Ryan.

We didn't see any boys, or any girls either.

'They're all at school, lucky things,' said Rochelle.

Jude and I looked at her as if she'd gone totally mad.

'Well, it's boring just hanging out at home. I don't want to get behind. Mum should have sorted stuff out, got us enrolled at new schools so we could start today,' she said.

'Oh, like she's really had the time, seeing as she had a baby on Sunday and her eldest daughter ran away from home today,' said Jude.

'Yeah, well, that's not *my* fault, is it? Maybe I'll go and find the school myself. It's in Neptune Street, Ryan said.'

'So that's why you want to go to school! Only remember, you're one of the silly little twerps in Year Eight. He's one of the macho retards in Year Eleven. I bet he won't even look at you in school,' said Jude. 'Well, *I'm* not going near any school. I don't see why we can't simply stay off till the summer holidays and start again in September.'

That seemed like the best idea in the world to me.

15

'You really need me to look after Sundance, don't you, Mum?' I said.

'That's right, darling,' Mum muttered.

'So I can't go to school now, can I?'

'That's right, darling.' Mum repeated.

I knew she wasn't really listening. She was clutching her mobile the way I frequently clutched Bluebell. Still, she'd as good as promised I needn't go to school. I relaxed a little.

Mum stayed strung up all afternoon, phoning Martine's mobile every fifteen minutes. Then she tried a change of tactics. She found out Tony's mum's number and rang her. Her hand was shaking as she dialled the number. She took a deep breath when Tony's mum answered.

'I'm sorry to trouble you, Mrs Wingate,' Mum said very politely, though she was pulling a hideous face as she said it. 'It's Sue here, Sue Diamond.'

She paused. Tony's mum was saying stuff. She didn't

sound as if she was making an effort to be at all polite back.

'Yeah, well, OK, I know we don't see eye to eye on a lot of things,' Mum said, struggling to keep her temper. 'But the thing is, I believe my Martine is coming to see your Tony today. Is she at your place right now? Can I speak to her? *Please?* She's not? You swear that's true? Oh God. Well, will you get her to ring me on my mobile the moment you hear from her?' Mum clicked the phone off and started to cry.

'Where *is* she? What if she's lost somewhere? I'm not even sure how much money she had on her. What if she's mad enough to hitch a lift back home? What if something's happened to her?'

Bruce heard Mum crying and shouted up to her. 'Look, Sue, I'll see if I can get my back strapped up in some way. Then we can go out in the van looking for her.'

He did his best, struggling off the mattress on all fours, but whenever he tried to straighten up he got stuck, hissing with the pain.

'Get back on that mattress, you silly beggar. You couldn't drive for five seconds and you know it,' said Mum. She paused. 'Thanks for the offer though. You're a real mate, Bruce.'

She started pacing up and down again, yawning and sighing and rolling her head around, her fluffy mules going *shuffle-slap* on the bare floorboards. Sundance wailed in my arms, wanting another feed. Mum didn't seem to hear her, though her nightie top got damp. She clutched the mobile, checking it again and again for texts, leaving her own messages.

'Please please phone me, Martine. I'm so scared

something's happened to you. *Phone me!*' Mum begged.

Then the mobile rang and Mum jumped, as if an electric current had sizzled up her arm. 'Martine?' she gasped.

Jude and Rochelle came running. Bruce shuffled back off his mattress to the foot of the stairs. Even Sundance stopped wailing.

'She's with you, Mrs Wingate? Oh, thank God! She met your Tony and walked back from school with him? Right, right, of course. Well, can I speak to her?' Mum paused. 'What do you mean? Of course I need to talk to her! Stop telling me how to behave with my own daughter! I *know* she's in a state. I wonder if *you* know the full story! Now just you let her come to the phone. Please! Oh for God's sake, you interfering old bag, butt out of things and let me speak to Martine!'

Mum stopped. She shook her head. 'She's hung up on me,' she said.

She dialled again. And again and again. 'Now she's not even answering.'

Mum tried Martine's mobile but it was still switched off. '*Why* won't they let her talk to me?' she wept.

'Maybe Martine just doesn't want to talk right now,' said Jude.

'At least you know she's safe, Mum,' said Rochelle. She had her jacket on now and her best suede heels. She slipped out of the room – and a second later I heard the front door slam. Jude looked up, but she just sighed and shook her head.

I hoped Rochelle wasn't going to find this Neptune school. I busied myself with Sundance, trying to show Mum she couldn't possibly manage without me. Sundance kept fussing. She didn't want me rocking her or patting her on the back or whispering into her tiny pink ears. She wanted to be fed.

'Give him here, Dixie,' Mum said wearily.

'I think you really should put him on a bottle, Mum, and then I could feed him all by myself. You wouldn't have to bother,' I suggested.

'Maybe,' said Mum. It was clear she wasn't listening.

'Martine will come back soon, Mum, you'll see,' I said. 'And then when her baby's born I could look after him too. I could be like a childminder to both of them. I could feed them and bath them and take them for walks in a double buggy and—'

'For God's sake, stop nattering, Dixie, you're driving me daft,' Mum said. 'Go and play and leave me in peace.'

I marched out of her room. 'I was only trying to *help*,' I said to Jude.

'I know, babe.' Jude was putting her own hoodie jacket on.

'Are you going out too?' I asked.

'Oh yeah, I've got a hot date in McDonald's with a guy with a diamond earring – *not*!' said Jude.

'You're not going to get in any more fights, are you?'

'Don't worry, I'm fully trained in all the martial arts by our chum Kung Fu Brucie,' said Jude.

'Less of the cheek, girl,' Bruce called from his mattress. 'I might be an old crock with a dodgy back but I could take you on any day of the week. You stay here and look after your little sister, do you hear me?'

'Yes, Bruce, I hear you,' said Jude, but she went straight out the front door.

'Don't you girls *ever* do as you're told?' Bruce asked.

I thought about it. 'Jude doesn't. Or Rochelle. Or Martine. But *I* do. Sometimes,' I said. 'Can I get you anything, Uncle Bruce? Cup of tea?'

'No thanks, Dixie. It's such a struggle to get to the flipping toilet I'd better severely limit my liquid intake, sweetheart. But you could turn the telly on for me if you like. I got it working before I did my back in.'

'You've got *everything* working, Uncle Bruce.'

'Except myself! That's a good little lass.'

'Any special channel?'

'Afternoon telly's all a bit rubbish,' said Bruce, as I flicked through the channels. 'Hang on, is that woman doing flower arranging? I'd better watch it. Iris hasn't got much clue – she just dumps each bunch in a vase, willy-nilly. I can't say I'm much cop at it either. It was always Mum's department until she got poorly. She'd got her Interflora and all sorts.'

'My mum's ace at arranging flowers,' I said.

We both looked at the flowers Bruce had brought us. The roses were arranged in the rosy china milk jug and sugar bowl, the freesias were clustered in the coffee pot, and the tall lilies were in water in the metal wastepaper bin.

'Well, she's certainly unconventional in her approach,' said Bruce.

'We haven't got any vases, see. People don't usually give us flowers.'

'I'll send you flowers when I'm on my feet again, Dixie. Flowers every week, eh? That'll make your boyfriends jealous.'

'Boyfriends!' I said, giggling.

'We could maybe start taming that jungle out the back too, plant your own flowers, eh?'

'But could we keep some of it like a jungle so I can play there?' I said.

I left Bruce to his flower-arranging programme and went out into the back garden. I felt for Bluebell. She was a bit bent over and squashed from staying shoved up my cardie sleeve for so long. I groomed her carefully, tickling her under her beak until her head stopped lolling and she started cheeping cheerily.

It was windy out in the garden. The long grass rippled like green waves. I played that I was sailing a ship in a storm, and Bluebell was a seagull flying ahead, showing me the way across the seven seas. After a year and a day's long sailing I sighted dry land at last. The seagull circled my ship three times in farewell and then flew away back to sea . . . and I stuffed Bluebell back up my sleeve because I'd got to the Great Wall of China at the end.

I leaped up and hauled myself up onto the top of the rough bricks. I sat there, peering over the alleyway into Mary's back garden. She wasn't on the swing today. She was just standing still in the garden, head bent, sucking her thumb.

'Hey, Mary!'

She smiled when she saw me, put her finger to her lips and peered round cautiously. Then she ran towards her gate.

I jumped down from the wall and ran to meet her. She was in her school clothes: a little grey pinafore skirt and a dazzlingly white shirt. She had matching bright white socks and big brown shiny sandals.

'Are you all right, Mary? Did you choke on those horrid crusts?'

'I was a bit sick.'

'No wonder! Your mum's so horrid to you. I hate her.'

'Ssh!' Mary whispered, looking shocked.

'Where's your mum now?'

'She's doing this big spring clean. I've got to play by myself until tea time.'

'I'll come and play with you.'

'She might hear us! She says you're not to come again. She says you're . . . dirty and rough.'

'I *am* dirty, sort of, but I'm not a *bit* rough,' I said. 'Everyone says I'm much too soft.'

'I'm sorry,' said Mary anxiously.

'No, it's OK. I wouldn't mind being rough. Anyway, how about you coming to play in *my* garden?'

'Mummy wouldn't let me.'

'She won't find out! Come on. I'll help you over the wall.'

'But I'll get all dirty.'

'No you won't. Look.' I stuck Bluebell in my teeth and shrugged off my cardigan. 'I'll drape it over the top and then you won't even touch the wall. Come on, Mary.'

'What if Mummy comes to see what I'm doing?'

'You can always pretend you were playing Hide and Seek. And if you're gone a long time your mum will get really worried and think something's happened to you. Then she'll be so pleased to see you safe she'll give you a big hug and forget to be cross.'

Mary looked at me pityingly. 'Mummy doesn't ever forget to be cross,' she said.

'Well. OK. Maybe you'd better not then. I don't want to get you into trouble.'

Mary thought about it. 'I'm already in trouble,' she said. 'I'll come, Dixie. I so want to see your house and what your bedroom's like.'

'I haven't really got a *proper* bedroom yet,' I warned her. 'Maybe we can pretend one?'

Mary looked baffled, but nodded happily. She carefully unlatched her gate. The spring was stiff and she scraped her hand, but she didn't flinch. Her little fingers were still red-raw at the tips.

'Why are you in trouble, Mary?'

'Mummy checked my bedroom when I was at school and she said it was an untidy disgrace. She said I didn't deserve to have such lovely toys if I couldn't look after them. She found my teddy under my bed and now she's thrown him away because she says he's all dirty and I'd catch germs off him.'

'She won't have *really* thrown him away.'

'She did! She put him in the dustbin and she tipped tea bags and milk and potato peel all over him so he's all spoilt now,' said Mary, sniffling.

'I think your mum should be shoved in the dustbin, she's so mean to you,' I said. 'Why didn't you tell your dad?'

'He's not home till I'm in bed. And when I've tried to tell him stuff Mummy says I'm telling silly stories to get attention. Mummy always twists things round. She'll say I threw my teddy away myself.'

'Still, maybe your dad will get you a new teddy?' I said, helping Mary up onto the wall. 'That's it, sit on my cardie. It's easy-peasy. Hang on, I'll climb up too. Let me get down the other side first, then you can jump into my arms.'

I swung myself up and over quickly. Mary clung fearfully to my cardigan on top of the wall.

'It looks a long way down,' she said.

'That's just because you're so little. It's all right, I promise you. You just have to give a little jump and I'll catch you.'

'I can't! I'll fall. Oh Dixie, I'm stuck.'

'No, you're not. Don't cry. Just jump. Look, Bluebell will help you.'

I stood on tiptoe and held her out to Mary. She grabbed her and clutched her against her chest.

'There! That's it, hold her tight. Now, all you have to do is jump into the air and Bluebell will flap her wings and you'll both fly straight into my arms. Just try it!'

Mary tried. She jumped into the air, clutching Bluebell, and I caught them both. They knocked me over onto my bottom but the grass was so thick it was like a cushion and we rolled around in a giggly heap until Mary started fussing about her clothes getting dirty.

She stood up, carefully brushing herself down. I helped her pull little bits of grass out of her hair. She smiled up at me.

'You're so kind to me, Dixie. I wish you were my sister.'

'I wish you were my sister too, Mary. I'd swap you with Rochelle any day of the week! Yes, you come and be a Diamond girl with us.'

'I wish I could,' said Mary. 'But I can't, can I?'

'Don't you worry, Mary,' I made Bluebell say. 'Any time you want to come and play with Dixie just hold me tight and I'll fly you there quick as a wink.'

She flew round and round her head while Mary laughed and tried to catch her. When Mary started to grab a little desperately I made Bluebell slow right down and give her an affectionate peck on her nose.

'She's tickling!' said Mary. 'The grass is tickling too!'

'Well, we're in the jungle, aren't we, so what do you expect? Let's look for animals, eh?'

Mary looked nervous, but nodded.

'Look over there, behind that bush!' I whispered. 'See the lions? What about that big fierce one with the mane? Let's hope he stays asleep! Watch out if he wakes up, he might be hungry.'

Mary peered at the old doormat I was pointing at. 'You can't have a real lion in your garden,' she said, but she gripped my hand tightly.

'I've got a whole *pride* of lions! There's a mother lion, see – she's with her little cubs. Look, they're having a pretend fight. Aren't they cute?' I pointed at an upended shopping trolley.

Mary blinked several times, waiting for the lions to materialize.

'What's that trumpeting sound? Oh, elephants! See their great flappy ears? Shall we give them a bun?' I showed her a broken umbrella caught in a tree. I reached up to feed the 'elephants' and Mary copied me, though she looked baffled.

'Is this a jungle, Dixie, or is it a garden?'

'Well, it's a jungle now. But maybe when his back gets better my Uncle Bruce will turn it into a real garden. Do you want to come and meet him?'

'I've got an uncle. And an auntie. They took me to Alton Towers and we went on scary rides and I screamed and screamed. It was my best day ever but I ate too much ice cream and I was sick in my bed,' said Mary.

'I bet that annoyed your mum,' I said.

I led Mary through the back door. She stared all round the kitchen, looking astonished.

'Where are all your units?' she asked.

'We haven't got any. Come on through.' I knocked at the living-room door politely. 'Hey, Uncle Bruce, can we come in? I've brought my friend Mary to meet you.'

'That's nice, dear. Of course you can come in. It's your house, sweetheart, not mine.'

I led Mary in and out the furniture towards the mattress. She peered around, looking dazed. She jumped when she saw Bruce flat out on the mattress.

'How do you do, Mary?' said Bruce. 'Please excuse my looking such a sight. I'm a bit of an old crock at the moment as I've done my back in.'

I squatted at the edge of Bruce's mattress. Mary huddled up beside me. Bruce tried hard but she wouldn't say a word to him.

'You're not very chatty, are you, Mary?' said Bruce.

'Never mind. I chat enough for both of us, Uncle Bruce,' I said. 'Do you want me to change channels on the television for you? We're going to play now.'

'Yes, I think I'll watch a spot of *Richard and Judy*,' said Uncle Bruce. 'I feel terrible hogging your mum's mattress and your mum's telly. Ask her if she'd like the television upstairs. I'm sure Jude could carry it up for her.'

I took Mary out into the hall. 'He's lovely, isn't he, my Uncle Bruce?'

'Is that a living room or a bedroom?' Mary asked.

'Well, it's kind of an everything room at the moment. We're not sorted out yet because Mum's just had the baby. I'll show you Sundance. I'm allowed to look after her.' I clapped my hand over my mouth, hoping Mum hadn't heard.

'I thought Sundance was a baby boy,' said Mary.

'He is. Well. For the moment.' I put my mouth very close to Mary's ear. 'But he might turn into a girl soon.'

Mary nodded. She seemed to be getting used to extraordinary things.

'We'll take a peep,' I said.

But as we went upstairs I could hear Mum talking in her bedroom. She was leaving another phone message for Martine. It sounded as if she was crying.

'She's a bit upset just now,' I whispered to Mary. 'We'll leave her in peace, eh? Come on, we'll go in my bedroom.'

Mary looked at the bare floorboards and the cardboard boxes. She walked round them warily as if she thought they might be jungle animals too. She sat on the very edge of the bed, dangling her legs. 'This is your bedroom, Dixie?'

'I know it's not very clean and tidy. I bet your bedroom's ever so pretty. But my Uncle Bruce is going to paint it for me when his back is better. And perhaps we'll get some new furniture. Jude and I want bunk beds. This bed's all rickety because we used to play trampolines.'

'Trampolines?'

'Yeah, haven't you ever played it?'

I jumped up on the bed and bounced up and down. Mary stared at me, shocked.

'Won't your mum mind you jumping on the furniture?'

'Well, the springs are mostly bust now, so it doesn't really matter,' I said. 'Come on, you have a bounce too.'

I pulled Mary up, holding her by her wrists because

I didn't want to rub her sore fingers. I gave a big bounce. Mary squealed, nearly wobbling over, but then she steadied herself.

'Shouldn't I take my shoes off?'

'Never mind! Come on, bounce!'

I leaped up and down wildly. Mary gave teeny little bobs, still squealing.

'Are you OK? We'll stop if you like.'

'No, it's *lovely*!' Mary gasped.

We bounced until we were both bright red in the face. One of Mary's plaits started unravelling.

'Oh, my hair!' she said, stopping still, nearly toppling both of us. She grabbed at her trailing ribbon, looking terrified.

'I'll do it up for you. I'm good at hairdressing,' I said.

I did my best. I couldn't get the plait *exactly* even and the ribbon didn't look quite right either, but I hoped it would do. Mary seemed worried about it so I showed her all the things in my cardboard box to distract her. She fingered my old animals politely, but their missing limbs obviously alarmed her. She stroked the cover of my fairy story book but didn't open it. She liked my fibre-tip pen set though, unbuttoning the plastic wallet and rearranging them into rainbow order.

'I used to have a big set of pens but I kept going over the lines in my colouring books and spoilt them.'

'You can colour in my fairy story book if you like,' I said.

'You can't colour in *story* books!'

'Of course you can. Look, here's the little mermaid story. You can colour the mermaid if you like. I'll do all the fish.'

209

We rested the fairy story book on the bed and knelt in front of it. Mary took the yellow pen and started colouring the mermaid's hair very carefully, curl by curl. She was concentrating so fiercely her tongue stuck out. I leaned over and coloured one fish purple with red lips and a bright pink tail, another one jade-green with royal-blue stripes and a third ruby-red with emerald eyes and golden fins.

'Fish aren't really that colour. They're grey,' said Mary.

'Yes, but grey's *boring*. And these are fairy fish so they can be any colour they want. "Bubble bubble, we want to be *bright*, please, Dixie," they're saying. And your mermaid's asking, "What colour tail am I getting, Mary? Orange? Purple? Navy blue?"'

'You're getting a green tail, little mermaid,' said Mary. 'And if you don't behave I shall smack it very very hard and lock you up in your bedroom, young lady.'

I looked at Mary. 'Your little mermaid lives in an underwater palace. If she gets locked up she just swims straight out the window, see?'

Mary finished her mermaid, I finished my fish, and we used both blue fibre tips to colour in the sea, Mary one side of the page, me the other. Mary's hand relaxed a little and she scribbled freely, her arm moving up and down. Then she stopped and saw her sleeve. She gave a little moan.

'Look!' she whispered.

There was a faint blue smudge on her white cuff.

'That's nothing. Don't worry, it'll come out in the wash.'

Mary kept looking at her sleeve. She tried licking the blue but it just spread a little.

'Your mum won't notice,' I said.

'She will,' said Mary. 'She'll smack me and put me to bed. And I haven't got my teddy any more. I can't sleep without him.'

I thought hard about it as I took Mary back through the jungle garden and helped her up and over the wall.

'Can I hold Bluebell to make me fly?'

'Yep! Tell you what, you can take her with you and cuddle up with her tonight. She'll sing you to sleep, you'll see.'

'You're giving me *Bluebell*?'

'I'm not giving her to you, I'm just lending her for tonight, OK? But hide her from your mum! I don't want Bluebell chucked in the dustbin too.'

Mary clutched Bluebell tightly. We slipped across the alleyway. I helped Mary struggle with the gate latch. I was scared her mother would suddenly come running and pounce on her, but the garden stayed empty.

Mary sat on her swing. She made Bluebell wave her wing at me. Then she quickly stuffed her right down the neck of her school blouse, out of sight.

16

My cardie sleeve felt horribly empty without Bluebell inside, pecking companionably at my wrist. I wasn't sure Mary would be able to hide her. I kept thinking of her mother hurling her into the dustbin. I saw her buried under smelly rubbish, unable to flap her wings and fly away. I saw the dustbin men arriving in the morning and emptying her into their terrible stinking lorry. I thought of her being driven away to the rotting wilderness of the tip. I knew I'd never find her again.

I wanted to tell Mum. She was huddled up with Sundance and didn't want to be bothered.

'But Mum, I'm *miserable*,' I whined.

'So am I, Dixie, so that makes two of us,' said Mum, pulling away from me.

'Can you just tell me what time dustmen come in the mornings?'

'Can I *what*?'

'Mum, I've done something silly,' I said.

'Well, go and tell Jude, Dixie. Or your blooming Uncle

212

Bruce. Leave me in peace now, for pity's sake.'

I trailed away, holding my fist in a bird shape, trying to make my fingernail feel like a beak. Mum started whispering to Sundance when I was out the room. I hovered outside the door, listening.

'We won't take any notice, will we, darling? We just need to be together, you and me, my beautiful boy. Yes, you're a smashing little chap. Look at your big blue eyes! My, you're going to turn all the girls' heads, but you'll still have time for your old mum, won't you, sweetheart? You won't run away, you won't get into trouble. You'll stay my special blue-eyed boy, my Sundance.'

'You're *mad*, Mum,' I said loudly, and stomped down-stairs.

I said it because I felt lonely and left out. Then I started to worry that it was true. Mum wasn't just pretending. She was trying to make it real. What if she never admitted to anyone that Sundance was a girl? Would Sundance have to have short hair and clump around in trousers and Timberlands for the rest of her life?

I went looking for Jude, but she was still out. So was Rochelle.

'Where have those girls got to?' said Bruce. 'I want to send one of them out for our supper. What do you fancy, Dixie?'

'I'm not really hungry, Uncle Bruce,' I said. 'Maybe some chips?'

'Chips! You need feeding up with some proper nosh.'

'I *like* chips. Mum always lets me have chips.' I paused. 'Uncle Bruce . . . do you think my mum is a little bit nuts?'

'Yes,' said Bruce. 'You're all nuts. I've never met a family like you Diamonds. You're all barmy, the lot of you.'

'Are you joking, Uncle Bruce?'

'Maybe,' he said.

There was a knock at the door.

'Let's hope it's Jude,' said Bruce. 'I'm not sure Princess Roxy-Poxy will deign to go down to the chip shop for us. Call out before opening the door, Dixie.'

'Who's there?' I called.

'It's your loveliest sister,' Rochelle trilled back.

'*Not!*' I said.

Rochelle was actually *acting* like a lovely sister. She'd bought a big bag of chips out of her own pocket money. She thrust them at me. 'Share them round, Dixie. Don't worry about me, I've already eaten.'

'With Ryan?'

'Yep! I met him from school.' Rochelle clasped her hands and twirled round theatrically. 'I was a bit worried about it. I didn't want him to think I was being too pushy. I thought I'd just saunter past. I decided if he was with all his mates I'd just give a little wave and walk on. He *was* with a great big bunch of them, those hoodie guys, though they look so different in their school uniform. Even the huge fat guy just looked like Mr Blobby in his school blazer. Anyway, Ryan came right over the moment he saw me. The other guys hung around for a bit, saying stuff. Some of the other boys from their school went by and wolf-whistled. It was dead embarrassing!' Rochelle boasted, dancing round the hall. 'I told Ryan I thought I'd be going to his school so he took me inside and I met the headteacher. He seems OK, and so I got our names down to go to the school, Jude and me. There didn't seem

214

much point mentioning Martine as she's not going to be here.'

'You didn't mention me, did you?' I said.

'Well, I did say I had this younger sister still at primary and they said you'll have to be registered separately. Mum will have to take you.'

'Don't tell her,' I said quickly, starting to tuck into the chips.

Rochelle wasn't even listening. She was too busy telling about Ryan.

'He understands *totally* what it's like for me, Dixie. He's part of this big family too, nearly all boys, and his mum can't really cope. Two of his big brothers have got kids already, one's inside and another is a junkie, but he isn't getting into any of that. He's clever, Dixie. He's got it all sorted; he's going to keep his nose clean. He's going to work hard and get good grades in all his exams. He doesn't seem to mind that *I'm* clever too – he doesn't see it as a threat. He likes it that I can't seem to help getting a lot of attention.'

Rochelle was showing off so much I felt like throwing her chips at her. She whirled round and round, swinging her hips.

'No wonder you get lots of attention from those boys. It's because that skirt's so short your knickers show,' I said.

'Ryan says he really likes the way I dress. He loves it that I wear girly clothes. He says I've got a figure to be proud of. Ryan says he's never been that interested in having a girlfriend before, he says nearly all the girls on the estate act like slags, but I'm different. Ryan says he's getting a bit fed up trailing round with that gang

215

of right losers. He's growing out of that stage. Ryan says
. . . Ryan says . . . Ryan says . . .'

My head was buzzing with Ryan this, Ryan that. I
went to offer Bruce some chips. Rochelle carried on
telling the empty hall what Ryan said.

Bruce raised his eyebrows at me. 'I wish her Ryan
would keep his mouth shut,' he whispered. 'Do you think
we could press her mute button, Dixie?'

We both chuckled, though poor Bruce jarred his back
and groaned.

We heard other voices as well as Rochelle's. Boys'
voices, out in the street. Lots of shouting. Then we heard
Jude shouting too.

'Oh no,' I said, hurtling out the room.

'No, Dixie! Don't you get involved! Look, I'll come – if
I can just roll off the blooming mattress.'

I couldn't wait for him. I flung open the front door. I
stopped dead, my mouth open.

It was the same gang, Ryan's mates, the Hoodies and
Big Fat Guy, but Ryan wasn't with them. Jude was in
the middle of them, holding up her fists, looking like she
was about to swing a punch at Big Fat Guy, but she
seemed to be stuck in slow motion. Then Big Fat Guy
brought his arm up – s-l-o-w-l-y – and blocked Jude's
punch.

'Yeah!' said Jude.

'Cool!' said Big Fat Guy.

They both laughed. The Hoodies laughed too and Jude
slapped all their hands in high-five acknowledgement.
She did an elaborate high-*ten* with the Big Fat Guy.

'See you around, cool dude Jude,' he said.

Jude came bounding into the house, grinning all over

her face. 'Shut your mouth, Dixie, or you'll catch a fly,' she said.

'I – am – gobsmacked!' I gasped. 'You haven't gone and got yourself a boyfriend too, have you, Jude?'

'No way!' said Jude. 'Are you totally off your trolley, little Dixie?'

'You're the girl slapping palms with that great big berk and all his gang. I thought you all hated each other.'

'Yeah, but their Neptune gang hate the Top Floor guys in Mercury even more. They heard I'd been in a fight with them, and that I'd punched their leader so hard he was knocked unconscious.'

'You didn't say you'd done that!' I stared at Jude. She grew upwards and outwards before my eyes, muscles bulging, fists encased in boxing gloves.

Jude put her head close. 'Don't tell, Dixie, but they've got it all wrong! I did swing a punch at the Top Floor guy but I don't think it hurt him one bit. He lunged forward to get me, I dodged and ran like hell, he ran after me down the stairs and tripped. *That's* how he hurt himself. But the Neptune guys all think I took on the hardest kid on the whole of the Planet Estate, so they kind of look up to me now. They wanted to know my fighting secrets so I waffled on a bit about Wing Chun. They think I'm an expert now, so I'll have to get old Bruce to teach me loads more.'

'Then you'll have to be very kind and considerate to old Bruce,' he called from the living room. 'And right this minute you can come and take supper orders. Maybe we'd better eat Chinese, seeing as you're so interested in oriental martial arts.'

'Your wish is my command, Wise Master,' said Jude.

217

She was in such a good mood that she didn't moan when I cuddled up really close that night.

'What's up, Dixie? You're a bit mopey. And how come I'm not being pecked to death tonight? Where's the bird?'

'I've lent Bluebell to Mary, to help her get to sleep.'

'That's very sweet of you, but duff move. Now *you're* lying wide awake – and so am I!' said Jude. 'You need old Bluebell more than Mary. She's probably got heaps more toys than you have.'

'Yes, but her mum takes them away. She's so mean to her. I'm not supposed to tell – Mary begged me not to, but I can't help it, I feel I'll burst if I don't. Her mum's so cruel and horrible.'

'Are you sure? I thought she seemed quite nice. She's too posh but she can't help that. So what does she do that's so horrible?'

'She threw Mary's teddy away. She said it was dirty.'

'Dixie, *lots* of mums do that. Most mums would have made you chuck Bluebell out *years* ago – *and* that awful old cardigan.'

'It's *not* awful! It's beautiful. And it still fits perfectly.'

'Yeah, yeah, whatever!'

'Mary's mum has done other stuff too. She forced her to eat her crusts and she cut her nails right back so they hurt.'

'Lots of kids have to eat up all their food and have their nails cut. It's no big deal.'

'Mary's mum says she's dirty when she's clean as clean.'

'That's not really being cruel, though. It's not like she's beating her or starving her or locking her up in a cupboard.'

'She does smack her.'

'Mum used to smack me when I was little, when I got into fights. It didn't stop me though. She doesn't smack me now because she knows I could smack her back, harder!'

'You wouldn't though, would you? Jude . . . I'm worried about Mum too.'

'You're a right old worrypot, Dixie. Look, there's only one thing you've got to worry about right this minute. If you don't curl up and go straight to sleep and let me have a decent kip too I'm going to tip you right out of this bed, OK? So night-night.'

I curled up and kept very still, pretending to be asleep. Jude started breathing heavily, her arms and legs twitching as if she was fighting in her dreams. I didn't go to sleep for a long long time. Then I woke early, listening anxiously for the sound of dustcarts.

Sundance woke early too and kept fussing, not feeding properly.

'Please try, little darling,' Mum kept whispering.

'Maybe he's not hungry, Mum?' I suggested.

'No, he's starving, poor little mite. It's all my fault. I'm all tense with worrying about Martine. I've lost her, Dixie.'

'No you haven't, Mum.'

'She's not coming back. She obviously hates me. I don't blame her. I'm a useless mum. I can't look after any of you. I can't even feed my own baby.'

I didn't know what to do. Mum wouldn't stop crying. Sundance cried too, and I couldn't quieten her.

'God, what a racket!' said Rochelle. 'I'm out of here. I'm going to the school over on Neptune to see if they'll

219

let me sit in on some lessons.' She was all dressed up in her shortest skirt and highest heels.

'What *kind* of lessons?' said Jude. 'How to be a mini-hooker? You can't wear that to school! Put your Bletchworth uniform on.'

'But I'm seeing Ryan. I can't let him see me in that old uniform, I look like a silly little kid.'

'Rochelle, guess what: you *are* a silly little kid,' I said.

'Shut up, you silly little squirt. It's a waste of time *you* going to school, you're so braindead you just get to sit by yourself and do colouring. But you'll come with me, won't you, Jude?'

'What? I've got better things to do than try to blag my way into a new school!' she said. 'You're crazy, Rochelle.'

Jude wanted to spend the day with Bruce, having intensive Wing Chun instruction. Bruce's back was a little better, so he could just about hobble around downstairs, though he was still happiest flat out on the mattress. Jude stood by his head, barely able to move for furniture, adopting the front fighting stance and practising an arrow punch.

I joined in for a bit but it was so boring doing it over and over fifty times that I wandered off by myself.

I trekked through the jungle, heaved myself up onto the wall and stared at Mary's empty garden. I couldn't see a sign of any dustbins. They must be kept round the front of the house.

I jumped down off the wall and walked along the alleyway to the end, wishing I had Jude with me. I made it along Mary's street and stood outside her house for several minutes, wondering if I dared creep up the crazy paving and search for their dustbin.

I had my hand on the front gate when I saw Mary's mother spraying the living-room window and then wiping away at it vigorously, even though the glass was already sparkling. I ducked down and ran bent over until I was sure I was out of sight. I didn't feel safe until I was in my own back garden. I didn't know why I felt so frightened. Jude had made me wonder if she was really as scary as Mary made out. Even if she *was*, she couldn't smack *me* or make *me* eat crusts or cut *my* nails or throw out anything of *mine*. She wouldn't really throw Bluebell into the bin too, would she? It seemed so awful she could do all these things to Mary, just because she was her daughter.

I decided I should get Bruce to teach little Mary Wing Chun too. Then every time her mum made a move Mary could block it. If her mum got really mad Mary could spring into action and whirl her way over her head. Then Mary and Bluebell and I could whiz off to Planet Dixie where no one could pick on us.

I so so so hoped Bluebell was safe and sound. I kept automatically reaching for her up my sleeve. I did a lot of colouring in my fairy story book to keep my hands busy but it still seemed endless hours until lunch time, and then the whole afternoon stretched out for ever.

I was waiting on the wall, watching out for Mary, from three o'clock onwards. I knew I was much too early to see Mary but I couldn't help it. I fidgeted so much on the rough bricks that I rubbed my legs raw. I heard a clock chime quarter past, half past, quarter to four, then four.

Mary *must* be home from school by now. Why didn't she come out in the garden to see me? She knew I'd be wanting

221

to see her. Couldn't she get away from her mother? Had she taken Bluebell to school with her, hidden in her school bag? Or had she tried to hide her in her bedroom? I thought of her mum shaking the duvet, pounding the pillows, opening every drawer and cupboard.

I was starting to think I'd never ever see Bluebell again.

'Fly home to me!' I whispered, and I looked up. There was Mary at the upstairs window, her palms on the glass. She was standing right up on the windowsill in her bare feet. I saw a flash of dusty blue in one of her hands.

I jumped down off the wall, rushed across the alleyway and climbed right over her gate. I crept across the velvety grass, nearer and nearer.

Mary stayed spread-eagled against the glass, wearing a long white gown. She was mouthing something. I couldn't see her lips clearly enough to work out what she was saying. I shook my head. She tried again and again.

I got as near as I dared, almost up to the house, craning my neck up at Mary. It looked as if she was crying. I realized the long white gown was her nightie. She was obviously in trouble again and had been sent to bed.

She waved Bluebell to show me she was safe. She held her to the glass, as if willing her to fly straight through.

'It's OK!' I mouthed. 'You keep her for a bit.'

Mary tried to reply. I still didn't understand, but I nodded my head to encourage her. Mary still looked very anxious but she smiled bravely. She started fiddling with the catch on her window. I stared up at her, wondering if she was going to try to throw Bluebell down to me.

'Don't, Mary! Careful! No, it's too dangerous!' I called.

Mary jerked the window right open. She leaned forward and put one foot out of the window, right onto the ledge. She was still clutching Bluebell in one hand.

Then I remembered my own words.

All you have to do is jump into the air and Bluebell will flap her wings and you'll both fly into my arms.

'No! No, Mary, don't!' I screamed.

It was too late.

Mary leaped into the air, her white nightie billowing. For a split second I thought she might really fly. Then she tumbled downwards.

I ran to catch her, my arms out.

Then she fell on me with hammer-blow force and the ground opened up and swallowed both of us.

17

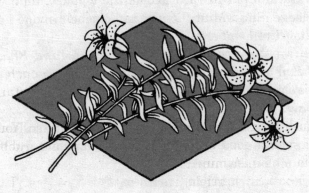

I could smell lilies, lots and lots of lilies, so overwhelming they were sickly sweet. I felt their soft velvety petals stroking my cheeks. My head throbbed, my legs felt weirdly heavy and my whole body ached. I tried to roll over but I couldn't move. I was held rigidly in some sort of container, trapped.

I opened my eyes and there was Dad leaning over me. My dad, who never came to see me. My dad, the embalmer.

I was lying in a bed of flowers and I couldn't move, as if I was in a coffin.

My whole family were gathered all around me. Mum, Martine holding little Sundance, Jude, Rochelle and Uncle Bruce. They were all gazing down at me, and everyone was crying.

'Am I *dead*?' I whispered.

'Oh Dixie, what are you *like*?' Mum said. She was laughing shakily but tears were pouring down her cheeks.

'What's happened?' I said.

'You've been in an accident, lovey. Don't you remember?' said Mum. 'You're in hospital now.'

'What did I do?'

'You went round to Mary's house,' said Jude.

Then I remembered. I saw Mary flying through the air like a little white angel. 'Mary!' I said, and I started sobbing.

'Hush now, darling, it's all right. Don't cry so. You've been such a good brave little girl,' Mum said, rubbing her face against mine.

'I'm bad, I'm terrible, it's all my fault,' I wept. 'I told Mary to jump off the wall and then she tried to jump right out the window and I couldn't stop her. Where is she? Is Mary all right? Oh please, tell me, is *Mary* dead?'

'Ssh, ssh, Mary's fine. There's barely a scratch on her, I promise you,' said Mum. 'Look, my darling, here's Bluebell. Mary said you had to have her back.' Mum tucked Bluebell in beside me, her beak nuzzling my neck.

'Where is Mary? Is she really really all right? Can I see her?'

'Well, her dad's taken her home now, pet,' said Mum.

'Her mum will be so cross with her!'

'No, no. I had a long talk with her dad. Don't you worry about Mary now. She's going to be staying with her auntie and uncle while her mum's in hospital.'

'Did her mum get hurt too?'

'No, but she's . . . she's not very well.'

'She's gone off her head and now she's in the loony ward. *I* think they should lock her up and throw away the key,' said Rochelle.

'Now, we shouldn't judge. Mary's dad said she's always

225

been bothered with her nerves, right from when Mary was born. It started off as post-natal depression.'

'That's just a fancy excuse. *As if!*'

'That's *enough*, Rochelle. It can make you do all sorts,' said Mum. 'You don't know the half of it.'

'I know she was being horrible to Mary. Why didn't you *tell*, Dixie?' said Rochelle.

'She did tell. She told me. And I just told her to shut up and go to sleep,' said Jude. 'It's *my* fault.'

'It's not anybody's fault. Don't be so silly, girls,' said Mum. 'And Dixie, you must feel very very proud. You saved little Mary's life running forward like that.'

'I caught her?'

'Yes, you did, you mad little darling. You took the full force of her weight. You were knocked unconscious.'

'Yeah, you've been in a coma, Dixie, and we were all starting to think you'd never come round and you'd stay a total vegetable,' said Rochelle. 'I felt so bad because I've always made out you were braindead anyway—'

'Rochelle!' said Martine.

'Yeah, but I vowed I'd look after you and nurse you and do everything for you if you really *were* braindead,' said Rochelle.

'I'm glad I'm not,' I said.

I tried to wriggle up on my pillows to look at everyone properly but my legs wouldn't budge. 'I can't move!' I said. I suddenly panicked. 'Can't I walk? Will I have to have a wheelchair?'

'No, darling, you're not paralysed – feel,' said Mum. 'Wiggle your toes! That's my girl. You can't move your legs because they're strung up in plaster, see?'

Mum slid her arm behind my head and helped me

peer at my new weird white legs, my pink toes sticking out of each end.

'They feel so *heavy*,' I said.

'Still, think how hard you'll be able to stamp on Rochelle if she gets on your nerves,' said Jude.

'How long have I got to keep the plaster on?'

'We're not quite sure yet, darling. Both your legs are quite badly broken. But you'll mend, sweetheart, and you'll be running around all over the place before long, you'll see. I'm going to stay with you while you're in hospital, with little Sundance. I'm going to have a mattress in a side ward – it's all arranged. I'm getting used to camping on blooming mattresses! But by the time you come home, Dixie, we're going to have your own bed all sorted, and we'll paint up your bedroom and make it as pretty as a picture. You'll help me, won't you, guys?'

'Of *course* we will,' said Bruce.

'If I can manage it,' said my dad.

'And I'm going to come visiting, Dixie. I'm going to be able to feed *you* little treats and help *you* drink out of a straw now,' said Bruce.

'Is your back better now, Uncle Bruce?'

'Yes, little 'un, it's on the mend now.'

'So are you going back to your own house now?'

'Well, I'm dashing backwards and forwards in the van. I'll have to see to the shop some of the time, but I'll come every weekend and I'll bring you lots more flowers. The nurses thought you were a little film star with all my lilies.'

'I'll come and see you too, little Dixie,' said my dad. 'But maybe not *every* weekend. I could bring my other daughters too. Would you like to meet your sisters?'

'I think she's got more than enough sisters as it is,' said Mum.

'How come *you're* here, Martine?' I asked.

'I came the minute I heard about you, Dixie – don't be daft,' said Martine.

'Is Tony here too?'

'No. We've had a row, him and me – *and* his mum. I got sick of them saying stuff, badmouthing us Diamonds. Bogging cheek! I'm not going back to Bletchworth. I'm staying with you lot.'

'My Ryan's here,' said Rochelle proudly. 'He's outside because hospitals give him the heebie-jeebies, but I could call him if you like. He wants to say hello.'

'No more visitors, please!' said a big friendly nurse, bustling up beside my bed. She put a thermometer in my mouth. 'Hello, my lovely. So you've woken up, have you! I think you might get a bit over-excited with all this crowd round your bed. How about just the immediate family staying?'

'We're all immediate family,' said Mum. 'I'm her mum.'

'I'm her dad.'

'I'm her uncle.'

'Her *favourite* uncle,' said Jude. 'And I'm her sister.'

'I'm her big sister,' said Martine.

'Well, I'm her sister too,' said Rochelle.

'Goodness, what a lot of sisters,' said the nurse. She looked at Sundance's blue sleeping suit and shawl. She winked at Mum. 'I bet you were glad when you had their little baby brother!'

Mum took a deep breath. 'Not a bit of it,' she said. 'Girls are just as good as boys. *Better*. And the little one isn't a boy at all. I just fancied dressing her in blue because I got a bit bored with all that pink.'

'Mum?' said Jude.

'Oh God, now Mum's gone nuts,' said Rochelle.

'Mum, Sundance is a *boy*,' said Martine.

'Well, I think my little babe's nappy needs changing, so have a quick peep and see if I'm right,' said Mum.

Poor Sundance had everyone peering at her little pink bottom.

'*Why* did you pretend she was a boy, then?' said Jude.

'I told you, she's gone loopy,' Rochelle hissed. 'And Sundance is an even weirder name for a girl.'

'Shut *up*, Rochelle,' said Martine. 'Mum, you said all along you were having a boy. It was all in the stars about your boy.'

'Maybe it's Sundance's *dad* who's the boy,' Bruce muttered.

'You're a much cannier bloke than you look, Bruce,' said Mum. 'I hadn't thought of that! Maybe I *have* got psychic powers after all.'

'I don't get it, Mum,' said Jude.

'I don't get it either, do you, mate?' said my dad to Bruce.

'Sue's a woman who's full of surprises,' said Bruce.

'If that's a nice way of saying I'm off my trolley then I'd have to agree with you,' said Mum. 'I *did* go a bit loopy, Rochelle. I couldn't even tell *you*, Martine. I suppose I didn't dare, because I knew you wouldn't keep it quiet like our Dixie.'

'Dixie *knew*?' said Martine and Jude and Rochelle.

I spat out the thermometer triumphantly. 'I knew right from the start, didn't I, Mum?' I said. 'Mum isn't bonkers. She just pretended a bit, that's all. Because she wanted Sundance to be a boy so much.'

'That's right, my darling. I just wanted to stay in my own private little dream world. But I couldn't. All you girls needed me. It's a drama every day in our blooming household – Rochelle getting a boyfriend, Jude getting into fights, our Martine getting pregnant. Then little Dixie damn near died and I was shocked back into my senses. About bogging time and all!'

'Well, Mum, maybe *my* baby will be a boy. Your first grandson, eh?' said Martine.

'We'll love it whether it's a boy or a girl,' said Mum. 'But let's hope it's another girl. Then we'll all be Diamond girls together.'

ABOUT THE AUTHOR

JACQUELINE WILSON is one of Britain's most
outstanding writers for young readers. She is the
most borrowed author from British libraries and
has sold over 20 million books in this country.
As a child, she always wanted to be a writer and
wrote her first 'novel' when she was nine, filling
countless exercise books as she grew up. She started
work at a publishing company and then went on
to work as a journalist on *Jackie* magazine (which
was named after her) before turning to writing
fiction full-time.

Jacqueline has been honoured with many
of the UK's top awards for children's books,
including the Guardian Children's Fiction
Award, the Smarties Prize, the Red House Book
Award and the Children's Book of the Year.
She was awarded an OBE in 2002 and is the
Children's Laureate for 2005-2007.

ABOUT THE ILLUSTRATOR

NICK SHARRATT knew from an early age that he wanted to use his drawing skills as his career, so he went to Manchester Polytechnic to do an Art Foundation course. He followed this up with a BA (Hons) in Graphic Design at St Martin's School of Art in London from 1981-1984.

Since graduating, Nick has been working full-time as an illustrator for children's books, publishers and a wide range of magazines. His brilliant illustrations have brought to life many books, most notably the titles by Jacqueline Wilson.

Nick also writes books as well as illustrating them.

JACKY DAYDREAM

Jacqueline Wilson -
The Story of Her Childhood

Illustrated by Nick Sharratt

Everybody knows Tracy Beaker, Jacqueline Wilson's best-loved character. But what do they know about the little girl who grew up to become Jacqueline Wilson?

How she played with paper doll like April in *Dustbin Baby*.

How she dealt with an unpredictable father like Prue in *Love Lessons*.

How she chose new toys in Hamleys like Dolphin in *The Illustrated Mum*.

How she sat entrance exams like Ruby in *Double Act*.

But most of all how she loved reading and writing stories. Losing herself in a new world was the best possible way she could think of spending her time. From the very first story she wrote, *Meet the Maggots*, it was clear that this little girl had a very vivid imagination.

Now her fans can discover a little more about Jacky herself in this utterly captivating, charming and poignant memoir.

'Literary superstar' INDEPENDENT

'A brilliant writer of wit and subtlety whose stories are never patronising and are often complex and multi-layered' THE TIMES

DOUBLEDAY
978 0 385 61015 5

SECRETS

Jacqueline Wilson

Illustrated by Nick Sharratt

'I keep a diary,' Treasure said.
'I keep a diary, too,' said India, and then she blushed.

Treasure and India are two girls with very different
backgrounds. As an unlikely but deep friendship
develops between them, they keep diaries, inspired by
their heroine, Anne Frank. Soon the pages are filled
with the details of their most serious secret ever.

A superbly moving novel for older readers from the
prize-winning author of *The Illustrated Mum* and
The Story of Tracy Beaker.

'The Diary of Anne Frank is woven into this story ...
this could have been a dangerous device for a lesser
novelist; Wilson carries it off triumphantly.
This brilliant writer still provides her fans with
reality at its most unvarnished' INDEPENDENT

A CORGI YEARLING BOOK
978 0 440 86508 7